Cair

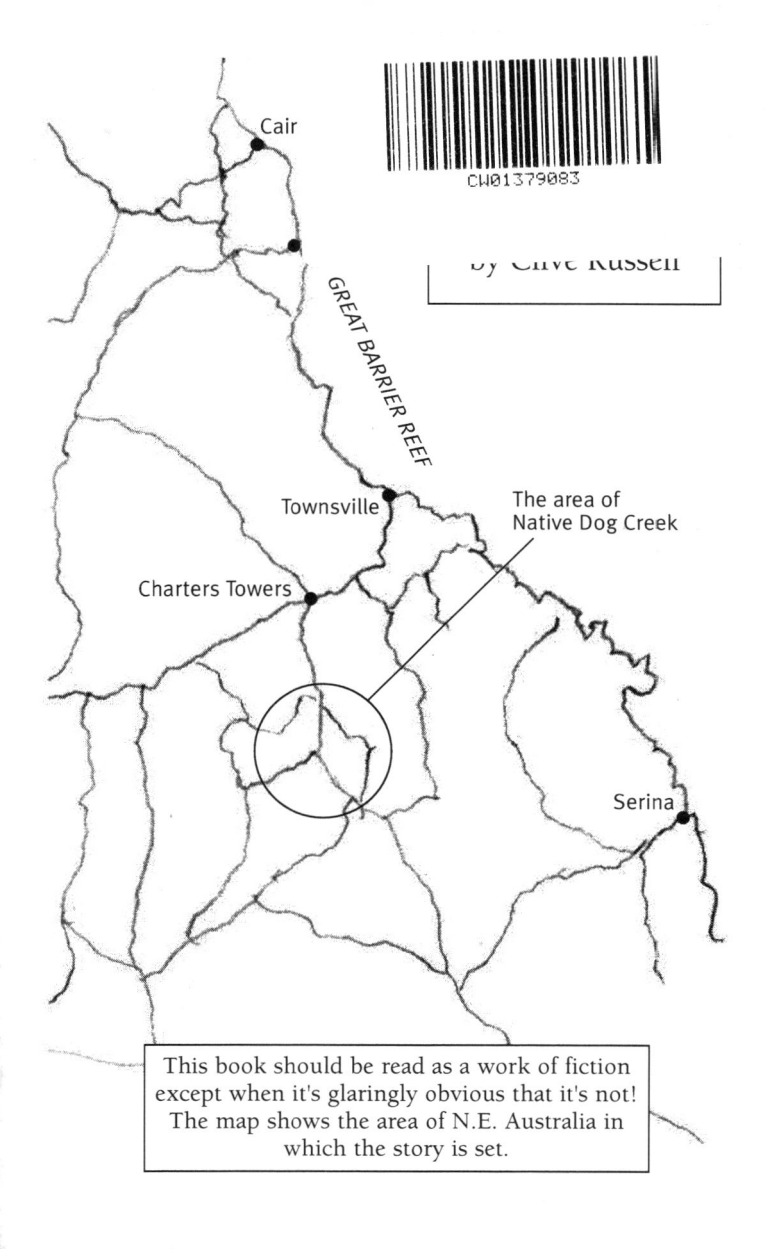

by Clive Russell

GREAT BARRIER REEF

Townsville

The area of Native Dog Creek

Charters Towers

Serina

This book should be read as a work of fiction except when it's glaringly obvious that it's not! The map shows the area of N.E. Australia in which the story is set.

My thanks to June Clifton for the use of her fabric art on the cover, to Pat Ashworth for her eagle eyed proof-reading, to Linda Reed for her infinite patience, and to countless other people whose ears I've bent over the years! And finally to Thomas Boysie Russell who might even, eventually, benefit from his Grandfather's efforts!

The Sound
of Silence

A story by Clive Russell

Brimstone Press

First published in 2010 by Brimstone Press
PO Box 114, Shaftesbury SP7 8XN

www.brimstonepress.co.uk

© Clive Russell 2010

Author contact: spikesdad44@hotmail.com

Clive Russell has asserted his right under the Copyright, Designs and Patents Act of 1988 to be identified as the author of this work. All rights are reserved and no part of this book can be stored on retrieval system or transmitted in any form, or by whatever means, without prior permission of The Publisher.

Designed by Linda Reed and Associates,
Shaftesbury, SP7 8NE
Email: lindareedassoc@btconnect.com

Printed and bound in Great Britain by
CPI Antony Rowe, Chippenham and Eastbourne

ISBN 978-1-906385-24-8

Chapter 1

'What's up then?'

The dog stopped growling as a caring hand reached down and rubbed an ear.

Emma O'Sullivan, a sound recordist, was downloading bites from a film track she had just finished working on and switched to the voice analyser. Seated at an adjoining desk was Paul Jenson, an assistant editor, and together they watched the frequency meters that definitely showed a speech pattern but there was no sound.

Various speeds and different frequencies were then tried on the analyser until Saffie gave a yelp and cowered in the corner. Evidently the dog could hear something so Emma replayed the track, cut the volume, then pushed the printout button and waited for the graph to emerge.

A few months earlier, deep in the inhospitable terrain of Central Queensland, a location crew had spent the day inspecting various sites for a film to be shot in the area. They were not having much success until, late in the afternoon, they came across an abandoned mining settlement which had a circumambience of calm, an almost pristine stillness, and it seemed surprisingly free from the usual vandalism of most deserted places.

The Location Manager, after a quick perusal of the site, felt that it warranted further investigation so he added it to his list of possibilities. Enquiries were made regarding the area near Native Dog Creek and it was found to be under the control of the Defence Department who were only too pleased to lease it for the film.

Contracts were eventually signed and then, after several weeks of preparation, the Director was satisfied with the site and work began. The outside shoot was completed on time, apart from the days when dust storms interrupted the schedule, and the crew returned to Charters Towers for the studio and editing phase of the project.

The Location Manager was then responsible for returning the site to its original condition prior to the lease ending. That was how it appeared on the surface at completion but, far below in the bowels of the flooded mine, the necrophilian equilibrium had been disturbed by the filming activity and something was starting to stir.

The truck came to a halt under a pair of gum trees, well clear of the main buildings, and on the only piece of hard standing to afford any shade.

Herb Miller jumped down from the cab, then reached back into the glove department for his camera; 'I'll take a few shots in case the environmental people get on our backs.'

He was referring to a pile of dusty garbage bags, some obviously savaged by the local wild life, that were stacked against a row of Portaloos. These should have been removed weeks ago and he made a mental note to phone the contractors concerned first thing in the morning.

'Do that and I'll get the flasks and a couple of mugs.'

Emma had needed to record some more background around the settlement. As Herb, who was a local man employed to tie up all the loose ends on this particular project was visiting the site anyway, the Director agreed to her accompanying Herb on the drive up. She didn't mention the unusual results from the graph that showed a definite voice pattern when there should have been none, but it hadn't interfered with the main sound track so the trip out was mainly to satisfy her own curiosity.

When they had finished their coffee Emma tied Saffie up in the shade before studying the site plan and comparing the area. There were rows of small cottages, most still covered in the dried silt apart from a few partially exposed structures, while at either end stood two larger buildings. One was marked on the plan as the bunkhouse, which doubled as the saloon while the other, a chapel, still had the scars of a makeshift steeple added for its role as the church during the filming.

Beyond the adjoining burial ground stood the industrial complex of steel structures associated with deep-pit mining, but Emma was more interested in the bunkhouse and paced it out with the recorder while Herb scribbled her remarks onto a note board. She then turned her attention onto the chapel before stopping for a break at the hottest part of the day.

The powdery red dust covered everything, even floating on top of the tea that soothed the parched throats and it was as they sat in the shade that Herb outlined the story of the site and the accident. A religious sect had been working the mine towards the end of the 19th century, quite successfully from all accounts, but it had ended abruptly one morning when a pocket of methane gas opened up during blasting operations. An underground spring quickly flooded the mine and the settlement's houses and buildings, clustered mainly around the pithead, became partially submerged and a small lake came into being.

The accident was eventually discovered far too late to do anything. However the local news-sheet felt duty bound to mention it while the stock herders, always on the look out for pasture and sweet water in such an arid area, avoided the sour water billabong that the lake had become and aptly named it *Hotskins*.

Any remaining signs of human habitation were gradually erased from the unforgiving landscape until the 1950s when the water table in the area started to drop, possibly due to the Marralinga Atomic tests. Sections of the higher structures slowly became exposed and quite recently a torrential rainstorm had washed away the silt and shapes of the past slowly emerged to become the present.

A few of the locals noticed the change but, as it was deemed to be Defence Department land, only a few hardy souls explored the site. The earlier oppressive and unfriendly atmosphere, coupled with the known horrific circumstances leading to the total demise of the earlier inhabitants, ensured that it wasn't considered for the *Local places to visit* brochure. Even the pilots of the aircraft that occasionally flew over the area didn't recognise any change and it continued to be marked on their maps as *'pit (disused)'*.

'Were there any survivors?' asked Emma.

'Not that I can recall reading about but you must remember that this part of Australia was in turmoil at that time with hungry and jobless miners everywhere.'

'Surely the authorities…'

'The sect evidently had no time for the non-believers,' replied Herb, 'and there were many stories, factual and otherwise, of weird practices and goings on not to mention the turning away of desperate and dying travellers at the fence line.'

'But surely the authorities…'

'The government can't even police the outback in modern times so what on earth could they have done then!'

'I know but it's just that…'

He looked at his watch, then at Emma, and struggled to his feet.

'I'd like to leave in an hour or so. It's the wife's birthday and I promised to fire up the barbecue.'

Chapter 2

'I just wanted to look down the mine shaft but it's as bad as before!'

During the shooting of the film the construction crew had set up huge vent fans to clear the gaseous atmosphere from the pit entrance but the air remained foul so the interior mine shots were done elsewhere.

Emma stepped out from the entrance and, with Herb following close behind, they moved slowly towards the swamp area dotted with brightly painted red warning notices. A temporary bridge had earlier been constructed, when the camera crew refused point blank to dangle over the swamp in a crane basket for the angled shots, but this had since been removed and the area returned to its quiet ambience.

'I want to do some readings around the fence line, then that other muddy part, and finish off alongside the burial ground.'

Herb's boots sank slowly into the slime.

'God! This place gives me the creeps,' he complained and expected a response but Emma seemed mesmerised by her recorder.

He walked back towards her. 'Are you alright?'

'Look at the frequency meter,' she whispered,' it's picking up a signal.'

'Of course, it's us!'

'Keep quiet then and look...'

It was certainly picking up something very pronounced but all Herb could hear was a very faint clicking sound like the rolling of dice on a board.

'It's definitely picking up a voice pattern again but not ours.'

'Are you sure?'

'Of course I am,' replied Emma and switched off the recorder.

'Maybe they're doing seismic shots somewhere and you've tuned in!'

'Don't talk twaddle. It's definitely audio and not geophiz!'

'I wonder if there's any magnetic influence.'

'I don't know...'

'If it's audio why can't we hear it?'

'It's out of our frequency range of hearing. Let me do a few more readings by myself, around the far fence line and the burial ground, and I'll see you back at the truck.'

'No way,' was the reply. 'Something scary might emerge from the bog and I don't want to explain your awful demise to the film hierarchy so I'll either sit quietly by the tower, on watch, or follow from a safe distance!'

Emma tightened the collar a notch, and then double wrapped the lead around her wrist. She'd had an idea to use Saffie so the pair retraced the path around the site while Herb followed close behind with the recorder.

Apart from the usual canine interest in her surroundings, Saffie showed no unusual behavior until they reached the pit entrance where she sat on her haunches and refused to move any further. Emma thought it must be the gas so they backed off and moved towards the swamp. However at this point Saffie shook her head violently from side to side in a futile attempt to slip her collar before chorusing into a mournful whine. Emma switched on the recorder, recognising the needle oscillations as if someone was shouting or screaming.

The dog's eyes were bulging as she strained to back away.

'Let me take the lead,' volunteered Herb, 'or shall I carry her?'

'No, I don't want to frighten her any more. Let's check how she reacts around the burial ground and then we'll head back.'

There were no further problems with Saffie as they walked along the path where only a few gravestones remained in a vertical position, the rest mainly broken and lying on their sides.

'It's certainly a haven for the wild life in the middle of nowhere,' she said, pausing momentarily and commenting on the tangle of creepers and bushes that seemed to have overtaken everything. 'But strangely enough it's not scary, just so very forlorn and sad!'

'Most of the inscriptions have been corroded away too,' he replied, 'which is a shame as I've got a mate who's involved with the local Historical Society and they've got a data base of all the old family names in the area.'

Herb then pointed at his watch causing Emma to smile; 'And firing up the birthday barbecue is far more important than exploring the unexplained!'

'Bloody right!' he stated and fell into step behind her.

Chapter 3

'Every knob has been twiddled and I've developed sine wave shapes unheard of in the profession!'

They were seated at a desk in one of the units of the small motel, back from Main Street in Charters Towers, which the company had taken over for the duration of filming. This particular unit had been rigged up as an editing and re-recording bay where Emma and Paul sat assessing the most recent recording.

'I've never known anything like it. Have you tried playing it backwards?'

Paul's humorous suggestion was meant to lighten the mood but Emma pushed back her chair and stood up.

'That's an idea, it shouldn't make any difference of course but I've tried everything else known to man.'

'Surely you mean woman…'

'Didn't I say that, I must be getting feeble in my old age.'

'I only meant it as a joke but if you think it might…'

'I'm out of ideas so let's try it. I'll hook up a converter and run it through that way!'

He picked up the end of a power lead then dropped it when Emma spoke; 'Leave that, I've got it sorted now so would you fetch Saffie?'

The dog had been obviously distressed during some of the earlier tests so, when her basket was moved from the office into the kitchen, she quickly climbed in and Emma hadn't heard a peep from her since.

'She was sleeping so soundly it seemed a shame to disturb her,' Paul remarked, leading in the docile dog and lifting her gently on to the couch.

'Yes, I know, but this is one way she can earn her keep!' replied Emma who then progressively switched all the analysis' controls to default before plugging in the unit as the sound of gibberish came through the speakers.

She pushed the pause button when Saffie started to bark, slipped her set on, and handed the other to Paul who plugged in both the jacks.

'There's something there so we'll save doggy sanity and use the headsets.'

With that Emma nodded and released the button.

Seated on the balcony of their unit later that day, they shared a bottle of 'Chateau Diaf 92' while trying to make sense of what they had heard. Having worked together on several projects over the last year, with a mutual attraction slowly developing into something deeper, they now seemed to be spending more time together. The nature of their jobs and lifestyles had affected most of their previous relationships so they were now adamant that their freedom was paramount and had no plans to change.

Emma had her own riverside apartment in Brisbane, inherited from her parents and which was only a couple of stops from Central Station, while

Paul lived nearby in one of the 24 units of a block owned by his mother. These units were solely for holiday or short term business letting and he bunked down in whichever one happened to be empty at the time. Each time he left for an assignment he cleared out the unit and stored the gear he didn't need in the basement. He could have stayed in the family unit but Princess Yi Eh Shaun, who shared the apartment with his mother and who had produced a dozen or so direct descendents of various cross breeds and genders, had taken over the most comfortable chair and treated the place like her own fiefdom.

Paul had no problem with a normal cat or two but the Burmese Tonkings had some odd habits, one of which was copulating frequently while meowing loudly to some ancient Eastern Asiatic dirge ascribed to Genghis Scan. These weird sounds didn't seem to bother his mother, she even used to hum along with the ones she recognised, but they drove Paul to distraction.

To avoid any confrontation with his mother, or the princess, he bedded down elsewhere and this arrangement, although slightly unconventional, suited all parties and that was all that really mattered.

Emma and Paul were involved in various advertising and media fields, both together and individually, although mainly on a casual basis which meant being on-call to a number of agencies in the City. In their personal relationship they had a lot in common but also a lot in uncommon. Once Emma got the bit between her teeth, maybe during a conflict of interests, an argument, or even a simple discussion with fellow workers, she seemed unable to back off with dignity even when it was blatantly obvious she had hold of the wrong bit, and this fact alone caused more dissention between the pair than anything else.

Food, however, occasionally was a close second!

Paul could eat or drink extensively without gaining an ounce in weight, and his medium height and swarthy complexion were at odds with his Nordic ancestry while Emma, who at 32 was a good 3 years older than him, only had to look at food for it to be immediately transferred to a thickening around her waist. With her fair hair and a healthy complexion, she took the utmost care of herself by keeping out of the sun whenever possible and using only natural skin products and cosmetics. However her weight worries were ongoing despite Paul's assurances that a little surplus was essential if they were ever lost in the desert. Adding to her concerns was the fact that on the 3rd side of the triangle was Saffron, a 4-year-old Blue Heeler Bitch who could, and did, eat anything dead or alive while still remain fashionably slim!

'If you hadn't noted the meter readings on site I'd have said that a stray track from another movie had somehow spliced itself in.'

'It's broken up into bits and the accents we heard from the analyser were not local, more like the old country with the *thee's* and *thou's* and *Lizzy Hapgood* whoever she might be, together with an almost American twang at times.'

Emma refilled the glasses and picked up her diary.

'I don't know what on earth to do. We've only checked a small part of the whole track and I can't really spend any more time on it.'

She flicked through the pages to the current month.

'I'll be finished here in a couple of days, then I'm booked to fly down to Brisbane on the Sunday where I'll have to clear my desk, after which I'm on to Melbourne first thing on Tuesday for that Media Arts Council Meeting.'

She jotted something down then asked; 'What about you?'

'I'll come back to Brisbane with you but I've got a dental appointment so I'll hang fire there for the moment as I've got a heap to do in the office.'

They sat in for a few minutes before Paul finally spoke.

'Let's make a copy of the original soundtrack and then, when we've time and space, we can sort through that reel and your recent effort.'

'I'll drink to that,' Emma agreed and lifted her glass.

It was a few weeks later, with them both back in Brisbane and that particular project quietly gathering dust on the shelf and others on the go, when the call came through.

'Don't you ever read your e-mail?' asked the voice.

'When I get the laptop fixed,' she replied before adding, 'who is this?'

'Herbie, Herbie Miller from Charters Towers!'

'Hi, nice to hear from you.'

'Are you currently employed?'

'Not at the moment but there's something in the pipeline. Why?'

'Open your e-mail and you will find something of interest.'

'Thanks.'

'Get back to me soonest.'

'Will do. How's the wife and the barbecue?'

'Fine, fine. Take care. Bye for now…'

'The Heritage Society of Central Queensland in conjunction with the Department of Mines and Boreholes, with funding from various Auriferous and other Mining Concerns, invite parties to register for a series of documentary films to be made this coming financial year. Employees and associates of either of the above concerns will be disqualified from applying unless a statement of intent accompanies the application. Ideas of film topics and locations will be welcome from parties wishing to participate in this project and an initial registration of interest should be made to:-

Mr G H Donaldson. Head of Media Studies. Private Bag. Brisbane. Q4000.'

To which Herb had added a footnote;

'I'm sure this will be of interest to you. Let me know if I can help.'

'We should definitely confirm our registration and forward our ideas.'

She waited for Paul's reaction to the information sheet from the Heritage Society outlining the terms and conditions when applying for funding.

He finished reading and handed it back.

'I'm due some leave but I'd only be interested spending it on the Native Dog project if we're asked to participate.'

'That's settled then,' she replied, 'we'll give it a go!'

Emma spent the next two weeks on intensive background research and preparing the application. During this time she discovered that the religious sect, who had worked the mine, had arrived with the Californian prospectors after gold had been found in Australia. They landed at Moreton Bay but the sect were soon targeted, and persecuted, by the more powerful religious groups so they left the coast to journey into the interior where they eventually founded a small settlement south of Charters Towers.

Their efforts at farming in the harsh and unforgiving conditions soon failed, but the discovery of gold at Gympie in the late 1860s was their saviour and they achieved a certain measure of success while panning the local creeks and rivers.

Underground mining was the next step having, by coincidence, the descendants of a large family of tin miners from Cornwall amongst their numbers, and eventually a steam plant was installed to power the ore crusher batteries and the associated equipment. Coal was dug from an open caste pit nearby so they eventually achieved a high degree of self-sufficiency and required only an occasional trip to town to sell the gold and purchase essential supplies.

From the newspaper archives Emma found a report dated February 1886 saying that the DMMC mine, at Native Dog Creek, had suddenly flooded and that there were no known survivors. She wondered who, or what, the initials stood for so she searched the Registered Companies Web Site to find that the company was still listed, under its initialled name, and had a registered office in Brisbane.

Paul persuaded her to call a halt, for the moment anyway, to her enthusiastic research into the subject that seemed to have taken over every free table surface in her apartment and affected both their lives to the detriment of everything else. She had more than enough background for the application, which was duly completed and posted off, but he knew from her inquisitive nature that she was far from satisfied and would continue to pursue the subject in the weeks ahead.

Chapter 4

'Please take a seat. Mr Epthorne will see you in a few minutes.'

Paul had phoned earlier on and now waited for his appointment at the offices of Abbott, Epthorne and Middlemarch, a firm of Chartered Accountants that also happened to be the registered office of D.M.M.C. Pty Ltd.

As he picked up one of the weekend supplements the door opened: 'Mr Jenson. Please come through.'

He folded the paper and followed the receptionist along the passage to an office where a tall grey haired man of mature years stood waiting behind a desk.

'Would you like coffee?'

'I would,' replied Paul.

'Two mugs please Linda and some biscuits.'

'I'm Tom Epthorne,' he continued and gestured Paul to be seated.

'I believe you're inquiring about one of our client's holdings.'

'It's at Native Dog Creek and I was hoping…'

'May I ask the reason for your interest?'

Paul explained that he had applied to the Heritage Society for funding to make a documentary film about old settlements in the area, and wondered if the company could help with any historical background.

Linda knocked and came in with the tray, quickly placed it on the desk then shut the door firmly behind her.

'Please,' he said and leaned forward in his chair.

Paul picked up the coffee mug nearest to him and took a biscuit.

'These are the registered offices and we submit their accounts in accordance with the law but any company information is available on the web so I can't help you much more than that.'

'Do they still own the settlement?'

'Again what I'm telling is on the public file but until a few years ago…'

He abruptly stopped what he was saying and walked over to a large map.

'Where did you say this settlement was?' he asked.

'About 100 K's south of Charters Towers.'

He sighted the distance between his thumb and forefinger, scribbled the co-ordinates on a piece of scrap, and took out a file from the cabinet.

A few minutes went by before he shut the file and looked over his spectacles.

'There is a 150 acre stock holding in that area but nothing about a mine…'

Paul took a sip as he tried to focus his thoughts then asked; 'Isn't that all Defence Department land around there?'

'Yes it is so maybe they would know more about it…'

'Did you know about the mine? I didn't mention it when I…'

'Hold on just one moment…'

Tom Epthorne interrupted the question by picking up a large magnifying glass and returning to the map.

'There it is, pit disused,' he exclaimed after a few minutes and motioned him over. The lie was so obvious that Paul sensed a charade, but he pushed his chair back and walked over to where the finger was pointing on the map..

'Thank you for the coffee Mr Epthorne and your valuable time.'

'Please call me Tom and if I can help in any way...'

'I'll leave my card at the desk. If the funding does come through then I'll write to the company, care of your good self of course, asking permission to go ahead with the filming.'

'Maybe the Defence Department would be a better bet...'

'I'd like to try with the company though, after all the mine's on their land...' He paused then asked; 'Incidentally, what do the initials DMMC stand for?'

Tom came from behind the desk and held out his hand; 'It came through the Register from way back as just that. Lots of companies use letters, or even numbers, but I've always known it simply by the initials...'

Paul shook the hand, thanked him again, and a few moments later was out in the street walking up towards Central Station.

'Don't drink all the beer. Herbie will be here at seven so we'll eat then!'

He stood to one side as Emma came out of the entrance to her apartment, with Saffie straining at the lead, and disappeared around the corner. Paul went through to the study where, on the desk obviously left open for his attention, was a letter from the Heritage Society informing Emma that she was on the short list and asking her to ring in for an appointment. It was attached to yet another information folder, so he took a beer from the fridge and carried it onto the verandah where he slumped onto the couch and started to read.

'I'm so glad you could come down as we need your help.'

'My annual check at the Veterans Hospital in South Brisbane was due next month so when you phoned I asked for an earlier appointment and here I am.'

They had debated about involving Herb further but agreed that his local knowledge and expertise would be invaluable in an increasingly puzzling situation. So while Emma fetched her folder, Paul served the coffee and nibbles.

'I've made a list of the points raised during the meeting with Tom Epthorne and we'd value your opinion.'

She handed him the paper and continued; 'We need to keep this between ourselves as it has the potential to cause a few problems.'

'Have you any spare glasses? I left mine on the kitchen table at home in Charters.'

Paul slid his pair across the table and Herb started to read while Emma laid out some cheese and crackers and poured more coffee.

'Fire away,' he said when he had finished the list and sat back in the chair.

'The Defence Department doesn't even own the land. So how could they negotiate a lease with the film company and did you know about it?'

'I didn't actually but it doesn't surprise me.'

'Why do you say that?'

'The place is littered with people's broken dreams. Visit any graveyard in the area and you will read of families, mainly from Britain, some from Europe, who came out mid and late 1800s and either died of starvation, or the heat, or just gave up hope!'

He leant forward and gave Paul back his glasses.

'The Land Registry find it a nightmare trying to sort out Miners Rights, Settlers Rights, Farming Rights, Crown Rights and any other Rights you can think up. As the holding is surrounded by army training areas, and was possibly requisitioned during the war, then whatever Grade 4 clerk who handled the initial application from the film company assumed that the applicant knew what they were on about and processed it accordingly.'

'Have you any idea of land description or what number the film company used when applying for the lease, I'll need it when we apply.'

'It's here,' replied Herb, producing a card from his pocket and reaching over for Paul's glasses again to read out the folio number which Emma then wrote down.

'I've got that now but what if I'm asked about that film at the interview?'

'Did you mention it on the application?'

'No!' replied Emma. 'Mainly because of what I had recorded previously during the earlier filming and to try to give a fresh enthusiastic impression of someone exploring new territories.'

Herb smiled at this and looked over at Paul.

'Does she give you that impression?'

'A fresh enthusiastic approach? She does actually but what if they ask how she knew about the place?'

'You accompanied one of the local guides, me, and together we explored an abandoned settlement which we both found very interesting.'

'But what about if...'

'Look!' He interrupted with an exasperated sigh.

'If they specifically ask you whether you have ever been involved making a film in the Native Dog Creek area, then you will have to answer in the affirmative.'

Emma nodded so he continued: 'But if they don't mention it then neither should you!'

She jotted a few notes then looked up, nodded again, and continued; 'You told me there were no survivors from the accident.'

'I didn't think there were although I've been wrong before.'

'If there were survivors then their descendents could be connected to the present company's board. Could you find out a bit more about it?'

'I'll see what I can do but I don't think I'll get far.'

'Any idea what DMMC stands for?'

'Don't know but I'd think the MC could stand for Mining Company.'

'Tom Epthorne nearly said that he didn't know there was a mine!'

'What Tom Epthorne might have said was about the mine on that particular property. The accountants, or possibly the company itself, could be involved with numerous other mines or joint ventures.'

'Can you find out?'

'Not really because most mining companies are cagey regarding their assets and tend to fudge their interests.'

With that he stood up and stretched. 'Is the cross examination over or do you plan to continue into the early hours?'

'I'm not that bad surely?' Emma said looking down at Saffie for support.

Herb answered instead. 'You're very thorough but I really must go as I've a lot to do tomorrow!'

'I'll run you back to the motel,' offered Paul and got up from the table.

He wound down the driver's window.

'Thanks again Herbie, but there's just one more thing.'

'What's that then?'

'I'll dig around Epthorne's outfit and associates. Maybe you can do the same as I've got a feeling they're not quite kosher!'

'Contact me if they don't check out and I'll do likewise.'

He waved as he entered the reception area and Paul moved off into the traffic.

Chapter 5

'I'd like to congratulate you on your résumé. It was well put together.'

Geoff Donaldson looked over the top of his glasses and smiled at Emma. They were in the interview room of the Heritage Society in Brisbane and Emma had just been called in.

'Thank you,' she replied. 'I find the outback fascinating but doubt if I could have survived the hardships that some of the pioneers encountered.'

'Quite, quite,' he replied then looked at the other member of the panel.

'How did you hear about the mine?'

The question came from Gwen Fortesque, a well-dressed elderly lady who eventually turned out to be the DCEO of Onesiphorus Mining, one of the several companies funding the project.

'I was on holiday in the Charters Towers area and got talking to one of the guides. He happened to have one seat left on the next morning's tour. And I really enjoyed it, particularly the old mining settlements, and thought how interesting it would be to be involved in a documentary before they disappear altogether.'

'What makes you think they will disappear?'

'Well they did once and may well disappear again!'

'Well said Emma!' enthused Geoff.

'Incidentally,' he continued, 'that guide wasn't Herbie Miller by any chance?'

'Yes it was. Do you know him?'

'We go back a long way and served together in Malaya during the Emergency. He's a nice man, a good friend too, but he sometimes had problems getting fires or barbecues going!'

Emma laughed but before she could answer Geoff gathered up her file to indicate that the interview was at an end.

'We've several other projects to consider so we'll let you know in a few days. Thank you for your interest.'

He smiled as he shook her hand and walked her to the door.

'I'll tell Herbie that you rang directly he comes in.'

Emma thanked her, put down the phone, and stared again at the letter opened out on the desk in front of her.

'Dear Sir or Madam!' Emma muttered to herself. 'Dear Sir or bloody Madam. Is that all they think I'm worth?'

Saffie looked around the room, knowing that she hadn't done anything to warrant such a tone of voice but, finding no one else about, wandered over and settled herself down by her mistress's feet.

'Not you Saff, just this Mr High and Bloody Mighty…'

Then the phone rang; 'Herbie!'

'It's me; the wife said you rang so when do we start?'

'We don't.'

'What do you mean we don't?'

'We haven't got the funding! A difficult decision, all the usual twaddle.'

They were silent for a few moments before Emma asked: 'Why didn't you tell me you knew Geoff Donaldson?'

'I know lots of people so why single out Geoff?'

'He was the one conducting the interview and it would have been nice…'

'Hold on one minute. Did the letter confirm that Geoff would be on the panel?'

'No, but…'

'Look you're upset. I am too…'

'I'm phoning your friend Geoff to find out why I missed out.'

'I shouldn't do that…'

'I turned down a two month stint in New Zealand for this job.'

'I'm sorry about that but…'

'I'm going to find out why especially since I worked so hard on the résumé.'

'I've just had an idea. Don't do anything at the moment and I'll phone you back within the hour.'

'Don't try and…'

'Make yourself a nice cup of tea….'

Emma put down the phone and saw Paul sitting at the table. She hadn't noticed him come into the room and wondered how much of the conversation he'd heard.

'You gave him a rough time and it's not his fault!'

'But I'm so upset after all my hard work…'

'All our hard work,' he contradicted, 'and Herbie must be just as upset.'

'I want to talk to Donaldson...'

'I'll put the kettle on while you do nothing until Herbie phones back...'

'Ever hear of the John Cowan Memorial Fund?'

Emma hadn't arrived back from walking the dog so Paul had picked up the phone and replied the negative to Herb's question.

'Well you'll receive an application form from the secretary of the fund and I want you to fill it in, copying the same resumes but don't mention the Heritage application being turned down.'

'She's coming up the drive now. Are you sure you...'

'I'm sure you can handle the situation admirably, so I'll leave it in your capable hands and don't forget to post that form away soonest...'

'I got the confirmation late yesterday.'

Her earlier irrational behavior had bothered Emma, together with Paul's further reminder that the Heritage Society application had been a joint effort, so when she received the go-ahead regarding the funding for stage one of the project the first person she phoned was Herb.

'I'm flying up to Charters Towers with Paul next Thursday and meeting the funding coordinator, someone called Basil Johnson, at the Imperial Hotel for afternoon tea and tabnabs.'

'Good, good,' replied Herb and then asked. 'Do you need me there?'

'No, not really, but if you can fax me down the hire costs of two trucks for a week, two drivers on

12 hour days, fuel for 600 Ks per day and mark it up 20% for the unexpected.'

'Can I arrange that myself?' asked Herb.

'Of course but it's got to be above board and on a checkable invoice!'

'Give me a ring when you get through with the meeting and I'll come over later in the evening.'

'One more thing before I forget. Paul suggests that I apply for a short-term lease to the Defence Department now. Can you see any problems in the light of what we know?'

'Not really. You weren't involved in applying for the original lease so you rightly assumed that everything was above board and if there's any comeback you can quote past practices etc.'

'Where do you think Tom Epthorne fits into all this?'

'I don't know but we can't worry about that for the moment.'

'I'll try not to. Take care...'

Chapter 6

'There's some activity around the site!'

The abrupt statement, spoken without the formality of a greeting or by your leave, made Emma turn her chair away from her desk to face the window. She had been in the office since earlier in the day and was discussing a press release with a colleague when Herb's call came through on her mobile.

'Who, what, why?'

'I don't know. One of the tour guides mentioned that he'd seen a test drill rig so a team may well be doing a site survey.'

'What can we do?'

'Not much but I'll try to find out who they are and what develops.'

He paused then asked; 'Have you heard from Defence regarding the lease?'

'No I haven't. It's been over two weeks so I'll give them a ring.'

'Did you get my estimate for the transport and catering?'

'I've got that but I wanted to tie up all the loose ends before I confirmed.'

'OK then. I'll hear from you later.'

'I'll phone Defence now!'

'Mr Khan please.'

'Just one moment.'

Emma doodled on her pad as the clicks and wheezes, so different from the music played to a waiting captive audience on commercial phone lines, continued until a voice answered—'Khan here!'

'Emma O'Sullivan Mr Khan. I'm inquiring regarding my lease application on the block at Native Dog Creek.'

'Oh yes-just one moment…'

Her doodling continued.

'I'm afraid it's unavailable.'

'Not available? Are we talking about the block LX1130?'

Mr Khan repeated himself.

'Can you tell me why?' asked Emma.

'The area has been leased for an undefined period.'

'Oh!'

'I'm sorry but you should have received a letter regarding your application…'

'I've received nothing, that's why I'm phoning. I thought it was just a formality…'

'I'm sorry Ms O'Sullivan…'

'Could you tell me who has leased it?'

'It's the Department's policy not to discuss individual cases.'

'You can't tell who's leased it then?'

'I'm afraid I can't but if they plan to do borehole tests then they'll definitely need permission from the Department of Mines—and all applications are open to public scrutiny.'

'So it's a mining company?'

'I didn't say that…'

Emma covered the mouthpiece as her thoughts went haywire. Maybe Khan didn't know about that specific mine being on the site and thought they were just prospecting the area.

'Ms O'Sullivan?'

'Yes, I'm here...'

'Sorry I can't be of more help but I will get an official letter off to you...'

'Not much use now,' exclaimed Emma but she thanked him anyway and put down the phone.

Paul was working in Tasmania but there was no answer from the hotel room and his mobile indicated no signal so she waited until that evening and tried again. There was still no answer so she rang Herb, who picked it up at the first ring and listened carefully as Emma related her earlier conversation with Mr Khan.

'I didn't mention the mine and neither did he...'

'There's nothing you can do about the application at the moment,' assured Herb, 'but we have to assume that a rework of the mine is on their schedule so we need to identify the usurpers and find out their plans.'

'OK. I'll pay a visit to the Mines Office and you ask around up there...'

The clerk at the counter shook her head and refused Emma's request.

'The applications are not in the public domain until they've been approved and the relevant fee paid.'

'What if the public voices any objections?'

'The approval is only the first stage—the public have 60 days to object.'

'Can they work the mine during that period?'

'Not really although they can do certain preparatory work but if any objections are upheld then the site must be returned to its original state.'

'How long does the application take from first inquiry to first stage approval?'

'Anything up to two months as we are extremely busy…'

Emma pondered her next move but the clerk spoke first; 'Will there be anything else?'

'Do you have the old boundary maps showing registered claims?'

'Yes of course but you'll need the folio number.'

She eventually found the information in the area plan book and wrote it down as the clerk slid a request register through the grill.

'If you can print your name and company, the folio number and the date…'

The clerk left the counter and Emma filled out the details then looked back over the folio number column hoping to find another LX 1130 entry. She found one, and there could have been more, but she only just managed to note its details before the clerk returned to scan the register's folio number.

'They are due to be microfilmed soon,' he said handing over the folder, 'and I'm afraid you can't photocopy them so please be careful as they're rather fragile.'

Emma nodded then quickly headed for a desk facing the wall and placed the folder down. Her hands were shaking so she sat and closed her eyes.

'Prioritise. I must be calm, inhale deeply. Prioritise.'

She silently repeated the phrase and breathed deeply before the agitation she felt towards the person who had previously accessed the file slowly subsided. The chair was quite comfortable and so, with notepad, an assortment of pens and pencils, and a large magnifying glass hastily borrowed from the office all laid out in front of her, she could now concentrate on the job in hand. From the information panel in the bottom right hand corner, she noted that the chart covered areas LX 1104 to 1139 with an update stamped April 1943. The area adjacent to the mine was obviously Defence Department Land, with its restricted access indicated by red marker lines and various decals, but when she zoomed in with her glass she could see that the line around the actual mine boundary had been whitened out so that two blocks actually appeared to be merged into a single block with the number LX 1130.

There was another attempt at whitening and her fingertips traced a blob, within the boundary lines, which she gently crushed with her nail. She blew on the residue dust and the faint number, SR 3318, was revealed on the smaller of the two blocks.

'We're shut from twelve until two but you're welcome to come back then!'

Emma looked up at the clerk speaking from the counter desk and then at the clock: 'I didn't realise…'

'That's alright Miss but we're closing now so please return the folder before…'

'Of course, I'll do it now.'

Paul phoned during the lunch hour and Emma quickly brought him up to date with her progress.

'Herbie might have a perfectly logical reason for looking!'

'Then why didn't he mention it...'

'Why should he.'

There was a silence so Paul continued; 'It's typical of a logical mind where all the bits need to be in place before it reaches a conclusion.'

'I know that but why didn't he mention it?'

'Were there any earlier requests for the folio before his?'

'I didn't have time to look...'

'Emma my dear. You must realise that we are only one of several projects Herbie will be involved in. I think maybe you should check if anyone else has shown an interest in the block over the last few weeks.'

'How on earth do I do that?'

'I've the greatest faith in your ability to confuse officialdom and don't forget to replace the blob!'

A different clerk was on duty when she handed over the folio request.

'You were in this morning,' he remarked and the opening was seized.

'Yes I was,' Emma replied. 'And I've got a bit of a problem!'

'Can I help at all?'

'I've had a run in with the boss regarding my time sheets and the dates last month. I was wondering if you could confirm them with the register.'

'Be my guest and check them yourself,' he replied and slid the book under the grill. 'I'll just go and fetch the folder.'

Emma took advantage of the opportunity and quickly worked back over the days prior to Herb's request. Folio LX1130 had been signed out a few days before that and Folio SR 3318 a couple of days later so she noted down those dates although the names and companies were indecipherable.

'Any luck?' asked the clerk who stood waiting with the folder.

'I was in the wrong,' replied Emma and returned the register to its current page. 'I suppose I owe my Mr High and Mighty an apology!'

'It happens sometimes,' replied the clerk and looked down to check the folio number—'You've forgotten to fill in this afternoon's request…'

A few more people had come in with enquiries so the clerk was kept quite busy. Emma took the opportunity to replace the blob of whitener that erased the original number once again and, while waiting for it to dry, she checked out the two dates from the register with those in her diary.

One was the Thursday after her application to the Heritage Society and the other was after Paul had visited Tom Epthorne.

The whitener was nearly dry so she ran her finger along the underside of the desk and artificially aged the blob with a sprinkling of dust. She was about to slide the chart back into its folder when another slight smear of whitening, this time on the

40

information panel, caught her eye. She opened it out again and held it up to the light.

The complete text was faint in parts but readable; 'Areas covered are LX 1104 to 1139 and SR 3318!'

Emma brushed off the chart and replaced it in the folder, then returned it to the desk and thanked the clerk before walking down the steps and out into the street.

Chapter 7

'I'll leave you to it,' she said and carried the plates through to the kitchen.

Herb had picked up Emma and Paul from the airport at Charters Towers and taken them home where his wife was waiting with a lunch of sandwiches and home made lemonade. She had set up the table in the garden, shaded by a stand of gum trees and a striped pagoda, and the couple did their best to make them welcome. However after half an hour Emma's agitation became obvious so they all moved back into the house where Marie left the three of them alone in the lounge.

'Everything seems to have gone against this project from the start.'

Paul opened his foolscap notepad to a fresh page and wondered how best to handle Emma's outburst as the tension between Emma and Herb was building.

'It's been a series of unfortunate coincidences,' admitted Herb. 'But let's go through the sequence of events and evaluate where we go from here.'

He paused and looked over at Emma. 'And first on the agenda is what's bugging you?'

'I'm sorry Herbie but why did you go to the Mines Office and not tell us?'

'I thought that was the reason,' he answered and leaned back in his chair as he looked from one to the other.

'Now I've got your undivided attention don't either of you interrupt before I've finished as I want to get one thing absolutely bloody clear.'

They glanced at each other somewhat furtively, nodded, and he continued; 'I've had limited dealings with the people from your arty-farty world of the media and have always considered them a bunch of stuck up tossers with delusions of grandeur. You two seemed to be OK though but lately you've acted as though I'm your errand boy which I'm definitely not.'

He looked again from one to the other, 'If this project gets off the ground, and I'm contracted for the transport, then I'll willingly errand myself around for you but until then don't either of you dare to bring my honesty, loyalty, or motives into question.'

He waited for the effect then asked; 'Do I make myself clear?'

A lawnmower engine came to life over the road, the noise breaking the strained silence that followed Herb's statement, and he got up to shut the window. Emma started to sob quietly, with her nose running freely, but neither Herb nor Paul felt inclined to console her so they let the emotion take its course until eventually she burst out; 'I know I deserve this but could one of you please get me a hanky!'

Herb handed the tissue box then went to the kitchen and busied himself filling and boiling the kettle before returning with a large teapot and three mugs.

Paul sat placidly, doodling on his pad and tactfully ignoring Emma's pleading glances. As far as he was concerned she'd got herself into this embarrassing situation by running off at the mouth and, from past experiences, she was more than capable of getting herself out.

'I'm so very sorry for my outburst but I've been…'

Herb put down the tray and interrupted.

'I'll accept your apology but don't try to justify your bloody awful behavior.'

'I'm sorry…'

'Accepted! Now what time are you due at the Imperial…?'

They talked and argued but it cleared the air and clarified some of the outstanding points. Herb opened the proceedings and said that, during his visit to the Veterans Hospital in Brisbane, he visited the Mines Office to check the old boundary maps accessing the folio number LX 1130 that the film company had used in its earlier application. That was the day after he'd had supper with them and, although he'd bought a pair of cheap glasses in town for the eyesight tests at the Hospital, they weren't much good for map reading and he felt the visit to the Mines Office had been a waste of time.

Emma looked at Paul and took her diary from her bag.

'You came down on the week after I sent in my Heritage Society application?'

'On the Friday and flew back later the next day. Why?'

'Two days before that, on the Wednesday, Paul went to see Tom Epthorne.'

'So?' asked Herb.

Emma then brought him up to date with her experiences at the Mines Office and had just finished her saga when the lawnmower engine started again.

'Just one point,' said Herb as he walked over and shut the other window. 'Ironically the whitener traces was the only thing I could positively identify on the chart without my proper specs but it must have been fresh or I wouldn't have noticed it.'

'Do you mean 'just put on sort of fresh'?'

'Yes,' he answered. 'And there's something else you should know…'

Herb sat facing them and said that he had been puzzled why the Heritage Society hadn't backed their project so he'd phoned Geoff Donaldson one evening last week. Geoff had initially denied any unprofessional conduct but when Herb told him to cut the crap, and threatened to find out why the funding had been denied by any means available, Geoff conveniently remembered Herb's tenacity during operations against the terrorists in Malaya.

After receiving assurances that the conversation would go no further, it was then revealed what had happened when Emma's application arrived in the office on the Tuesday. Geoff had taken it home that evening to read and found it to be a well-researched piece of work that fitted the criteria exactly so he approved it 100%. Next morning he passed it on to Gwen Fortescue, who represented the mining interests and therefore most of the funding, but a few days later she declined to comment adding that they shouldn't commit themselves at that early stage.

This change of attitude surprised Geoff; he had always got on well with Gwen in the past, but from that point on she seemed to make a point of avoiding him and he'd had little contact with her since. Emma had conducted herself very professionally at the interview and he was gob-smacked, to say the least, when Gwen stonewalled the application and supported some half-baked scheme from a bunch of students at Winton.

He later tackled Gwen about this and all she said was that Emma seemed rather flighty during the interview and not quite up to the job. When he tried to argue the case she reminded him, quite bluntly in fact, that her own mining companies and the others she represented provided the money and support for these schemes so they had the last say on who did what.

Even the Society's Secretary sympathised with him but was unable to interfere with the decision. Geoff added that he felt awful but as the Heritage Society relied heavily on financial support from the mining sector, he had to act diplomatically regarding the projects funded by external grants.

Emma looked at her diary again when Herb had finished speaking.

'So the same someone looked at the chart the day after Gwen got my application and again on the day after Paul visited Tom Epthorne. It's a good chance then that the original boundary lines were erased on one of those occasions before Herbie checked them.'

'Are you sure it's the same someone?' asked Paul.

'The scribbles in the Mines Register were similar and if someone had contacted Defence to enquire what folio number the mine came under, then LX1130 would have been given because that's how it's still listed on their books. I've got that funny feeling that both Tom and Gwen could both emerge as the probable front runners in this saga.'

Herb got up to open both the windows as Emma continued; 'Khan wouldn't have known about any deception when they applied for the lease. He'd just assume that the applicant was interested in that particular area and he really had no reason to check otherwise. And I'd bet that Tom Epthorne would have been the only one who would have still referred to the block as SR 3318 because this number would have been on the original paperwork and that was before he'd got around to doctoring the file.'

'Why go through the charade of altering the boundary lines?' Paul asked. 'Surely he could have applied direct to the DMMCs board for a lease.'

'They could well have a religious bent,' answered Herb, 'and still regard the mine as a burial site so Defence could have been the easiest option for the mining company seeing as a short term lease to the film company had earlier been granted with no problems. And they will only be paying a peppercorn rental as most of that training area is disused at present. Australian Forces are mainly concerned with peacekeeping duties so with the automatic right of renewal for present lessees…'

'And don't forget,' interrupted Emma, 'that the folios will soon go underground and out of reach after they've been microfilmed, so if the original boundary had been erased...'

Herb paused and looked at his watch. 'I'd better get you down to the Imperial Hotel for that meeting.'

'It's quite a lot to digest in one go,' remarked Paul as Herb walked them out to the car. 'And a few loose ends need to be tied up before we leave so I'll phone you after the meeting.'

Herb was sitting in the lobby, and just about to bite into one of the delicious hot rolls served gratis with coffee to the associates of the guests, when Paul walked in from the street. Emma had rung Herb early the previous evening to invite the couple out for dinner but his wife wasn't up to it so he agreed to join her for breakfast the next morning. She hadn't mentioned any details of the meeting with Basil, or any of the people from the Fund, except to say it had gone well and that the project might soon be up and running.

'Emma will be down in a few minutes but I have to get back to Brisbane so I'll be in touch or whatever...'

'She sounded quite positive last night. What happened?'

'Wait until she comes down as she wants to tell you herself.'

'Why all the secrecy...'

'I promised. My lips are sealed...'

'And another pot of coffee please.'

The waitress gathered the menu cards as Emma shook out her napkin.

'He confirmed funding this morning…'

'Will the company give us access to the site?'

'Basil's a nice guy, well up on the play regarding mining, and guarantees it. They haven't got through the application stage and then there's another 60 days…'

'What if they refuse,' asked Herb although he knew the reputation of the man in question was above reproach.

'I don't think they will as he happens to be the safety surveyor for several of the insurance companies and he could make life very awkward for that particular one.'

Herb remembered that Basil Johnson's best friend had been killed, along with two others, when the ratchet pawl on a lift winding mechanism failed. It was fitted to stop the cage when the electric power was interrupted and the mine manager had signed that it had been tested monthly.

An inspection after the tragedy however found the pawl to be inoperative, and had been for some time, so the manager was charged with manslaughter but he'd only served 12 months in prison. Basil Johnson took it on himself, almost a one-man crusade, to make the mining companies more accountable. The John Cowan Trust Fund had been set up and the subject of Emma's project, the filming of a documentary in the general area where the horrific accident had occurred, must have appealed to the powers that be and funding was approved.

'So where do we go from here?' asked Herb pouring out more juice.

'Mr Johnson will liaise with the company, on our behalf, regarding access to the site. And he's waiting on a set of insurance indemnity documents to be faxed up which any of our team working out there will have to sign.'

Emma took out her diary. 'I've earmarked a ten-day slot starting a week on Sunday. Paul should be clear of his commitments by then and a friend of mine, a cameraman named Jeff Saunders, will complete the team.'

She topped up her cup from the elegant coffeepot and looked up.

'And we won't be able to afford to stay here so could you book us into a motel with an extra unit to store our gear and set up the office equipment.'

'I know just the place and I think they've already got a utility room set up.'

'That's good.'

'When are you returning to Brisbane?'

'Later this evening. I've got to see Basil and a few other people before then.'

'Will you need me...?'

'Not this time but I'll freight the gear up next week to arrive at the local depot on Thursday. I'll put you on pay from then so book the utility room from that day and the three units from the Saturday.'

Herb stood up and looked at his watch.

'That's fine with me. I've got a tour party at ten o'clock and we'll be passing Native Dog Creek so I'll give the mine a once over.'

Emma picked up the bill.

'Thanks again and I'm sorry about the misunderstanding...'

'No misunderstanding, you were just bloody difficult…'

'Your attitude will take a turn for the better as from next Thursday!'

'Of course Madam,' smiled Herb and smartly clicked his heels before heading for the door.

Chapter 8

'Pleased to see you again Paul, would you like coffee?'

The phone call on the day after he'd arrived back in Brisbane, asking him to call at his earliest convenience, came out of the blue so Paul delayed a visit to the Government Library and was ushered straight into Tom Epthorne's office. Linda brought in a tray and a few minutes later Tom appeared and sat down at his desk.

After the coffee had been poured, a selection of biscuits dispensed from the tin and the door firmly shut, Tom eased himself back into the chair.

'Since I spoke to you the last time there has been a development that might interest you regarding access to the mine for your filming project.'

He bit into a digestive and continued; 'A company has taken a lease on the mine, purely for assessment and exploratory work, and they may allow you and your team limited access.'

'Under certain conditions of course,' he added almost as an after-thought.

'How did they know about the project?' asked Paul.

Tom shifted uncomfortably in his seat.

'I don't know exactly, as the Defence Department seems to be handling it at the moment, but if you contact them then they can take it from there.'

'So the DMMC must have come to an arrangement with the Department?'

He shifted even more uncomfortably and turned to look out of the window.

'As I said I don't know exactly, but that's really no concern of yours.'

Paul looked up sharply but held his tongue and stood up.

'Thank you for your time and the information Mr Epthorne and I'll let you get on with your real work.'

'Not at all. I'll fax you the details regarding site access and feel free to call at any time.'

Paul shook the offered hand, nodded to Linda on his way out, and was soon on his way down to the Archives.

'Epthorne knew about the Trust giving us funding and appeared to condone the Defence Department handling DMMC affairs. He gave the impression that the permission to film was coming from him.'

'Sort of keeping ones adversaries within arms length.'

'The Defence requisitioned lots of odd tracts of land for the duration of hostilities but it was all supposed to have been handed back after the war.'

They were sitting in Emma's lounge, going over the interviews with both Basil and Tom, and when Paul paused she took a folder from her briefcase.

'There was something else I came across; I think it recently came down from Herbie...'

She shuffled through some papers. 'Yes, quote; *DMMC will definitely not allow any re-opening of the mine as their grandparents still remain entombed below ground and they consider it a sacred burial site.*'

'What date's on that?' Paul asked.

'None that I can see but it's fairly recent.'

'These members of the DMMC then, whoever they may be, could well be the offspring of the survivors whose parents died in the disaster. If they're still alive then they must be quite ancient.'

'In their 90s at least!'

'Does it say who actually survived then?'

The papers were further shuffled until Emma found those details; 'A couple of men loading coal at the open coal face, a pony boy handling the cart, and a young girl moving some cattle.'

'But the other reports stated that the whole community perished.'

'It wasn't reported initially in the press until months afterwards so the bit about the survivors could have been even later when it was old news.'

'I wonder who's on the board of DMMC now.'

'Herbie's promised to carry on searching the records when he has time to spare which isn't very often.'

'Of course,' mused Paul. 'We do have the ethical aspect of this to consider as our silence could be construed as assisting a mining company in a fraudulent act...'

'Don't you even mention ethics and mining companies in the same breath...'

At that moment Saffie pushed open the kitchen door and walked into the lounge carrying the empty bowl in her mouth; 'Looks like she's trying to tell us something,' laughed Emma. 'I'll feed her and then you can take me to the Occidental for lunch!'

Chapter 9

'We won't be venturing far from the cage but the breathing tubes are there to use if you need them.'

The pair, safely kitted out in waterproof overalls, hard hats, and boots, nodded and stood back as Jim Saidler shut the steel doors, swung over the safety bars, and moved the directional control to engage the lowering gear. As the cage descended into the gloom the damp condensate, rising from the salvage pumps working intermittently to control the water level, stung Emma's throat.

She clipped on the gauze facemask and switched on her torch that illuminated the shaft sides and rock formations. It was frightening and fascinating all at once and the algae, shimmering with phosphorescence and damp with moisture, all added to the effect.

They had arrived in Charters Towers at midday on Saturday and went straight to 'The Fountain Court Motel' where Herb had booked them in. The utility room was soon transformed into the office facility and once that was up and running, the filming equipment was assembled and tested so it was the early hours of the Sunday before they finally climbed into bed.

It was Basil, all very bright and breezy, who came knocking at nine o'clock later that morning to disturb their peace and asked if they would like to accompany him to the mine.

'Give me five minutes to dress and I'll be with you.'

Emma was enthusiastic but Paul was not satisfied with the lighting and camera gear so he decided to stay behind with Jeff, the third member of the filming team, to iron out the problems as everything had to be ready for the Monday morning start.

Basil had arranged to pick up Herb on the way and when they arrived at his house they found him waiting with enough sandwiches, fruit and boiled eggs to feed a battalion. Marie had prepared them 'just in case' so, after these had been loaded together with yet another extra jerry can of fuel, they then proceeded south on the hot and dusty journey.

When a high wire security fence, only recently installed and completely sealing off the area, came into view just after midday everyone breathed a sigh of relief but it still took ten minutes of horn honking at the main gate before someone appeared.

'How do,' the someone ventured in a strong Yorkshire accent as he unlocked the bars and pulled open the gates. Jim Saidler was the Site Engineer originally from Barnsley so Basil, who had known Jim for a few years, made the introductions.

'I'd like you to meet Emma O'Sullivan and you know Herbie of course.'

They both nodded and Basil continued; 'Could you take care of them Jim? A look around the site and Emma particularly wants to go down to the first level gallery.'

'They'll need to sign the insurance indemnity sheets first and then I'll sort out some protective gear.'

'I've got the forms here,' replied Basil and clicked open the catches on his briefcase. 'I'll wait in the office...'

The cage shuddered as it braked and finally came to a halt. A violet strobe light came on as he opened the doors and he said, before disappearing into the gloom; 'Wait here for a moment while I do a couple of safety checks.'

Herb zipped up his jacket and stood beside Emma. 'Is it as you expected?'

'I don't know what I expected but it certainly wasn't this!' She attempted to sound confident, albeit unsuccessfully, while trying to control her involuntary shaking at finding herself suddenly plunged below ground into such a frightening and awesome atmosphere, that seemed to retain the memory of every shovelful wrought from the depths below.

They shone their torches up at the huge roof and cross beam supports and were about to comment on their almost pristine condition when Jim reappeared and read their thoughts.

'It surprises everyone who's been down here. The water must've had some protective elements dissolved that acted as a preservative.'

'Those boilers over there Jim!' Herb indicated with his torch at a large round inspection plate on the side of an even larger vertical cylindrical structure that seemed to be sprinkled with glittering black.

'There are three old Roscommon Uprights to drive the conveyor and the crusher. Gravity fed from the coal shute above and they seem OK externally but I can't vouch for the innards.'

'Is the area safe?' Emma enquired, returning to the matter in hand but knowing full well that her voice was one octave above the norm as she struggled to control her growing sense of unease.

'Don't you worry Miss, it's quite daunting but it is safe and you'll soon get used to it.' The Engineer even went as far as patting Emma on the arm but his assurances did nothing to relax her aching jaw or, to a greater degree, ease her clenched buttocks!

'If the air smells suddenly clean and fresh then return to the cage at once and suck on one of those tubes.'

'Why's that then Mr Saidler?' Emma asked.

'Some of the marsh gas found below ground initially neutralises the brain part of our sense of smell and hanging around too long in that area could kill you,' he replied and continued; 'Anyway I'll blow three blasts on the hooter in case of a minor problem and a continuous blast when the fifteen minutes are up. If there's a major problem I'll pull the pin on the air klaxon that'll shatter your eardrums. Don't lose sight of the strobe light and, if it speeds up, return to base. Stay on the duckboards and I'll be in the cage finishing my crossword!'

They stood and watched as he made his way back before turning and making their own way tentatively along the boards. After a few steps Herb noticed

Emma's hesitancy so he paused to ask: 'Are you sure you're OK?'

'Not really and I can't blame it on claustrophobia but I just feel so bloody helpless in such a vast area where so many lives were extinguished on that morning, and where their souls were never properly laid to rest.'

She shone her torch around the bottom of the walls as if searching for something.

'They must have found bits of bodies, or skulls, or clothing, or tools.'

'Any human remains would have been carefully collected and whisked away for a midnight internment within a quiet country churchyard.'

'I didn't hear anything about…'

'You wouldn't as the last thing a mining company needed on their main gate was a possible ancient burial site notice posted upon it!'

'It's just that…'

'And if the Commission had declared it a sacred site with possible indigenous links, citing that the locals might have been involved in some way and could possibly have been working in the mine, then that would have really spiked their guns!'

But surely…'

'Nothing you can do about it now,' Herb assured her then quickly added: 'If you want to go back it's OK by me.'

'If I caved in now I'd seriously regret it for the rest of my natural. So just put up with my chattering teeth, and the sweet smell of abject fear, and let's carry on with our Sunday Afternoon Tour.'

Low wattage safety lamps illuminated the gallery with sturdy ropes and posts slung along the route for handholds. They felt safe and as their confidence increased so did their interest.

'They've had the water blasters down here and they've done a good job,' exclaimed Herb as a steam generator and a conveyor system, both stripped clean of algae growth, came into view and under his scrutiny.

When Emma didn't reply he looked over towards her, saw that she had uncased her audiometer, and asked; 'Should you be...?'

'It's intrinsically safe,' she interrupted and handed over her torch then switched the unit on.

Herb lowered his torch illuminating the dial and control knobs as Emma filtered out the background noise to zero the needle.

'I might as well try the magnetometer then,' said Herb, 'just to check the field strengths but I'll break my neck if I walk around here with my eyes down so I've set a buzzer to sound if anything unusual kicks in.'

Further along the gallery a side clearing led off to a small circle of standing stones, each about two metres in height and pear shaped with the widest part at the top and the bottom end set into the rock. There were ten in all and, while they stood wondering about their purpose or significance, a burst of light like a miniature starshell flashed from the top of the nearest one.

Suddenly the magnetometer's buzzer sounded and rumbling noises, like an oncoming train away in the distance, broke through the silence while a sudden explosion within the standing stone nearby knocked them further down the tunnel and a flying pit prop hit Herb on the leg.

Her screams went unheard as a klaxon started to wail followed by a loud crash that plunged the gallery into darkness. Herb scrabbled frantically around on one knee, searching for the torches they had both dropped, and he eventually found them then helped Emma to her feet.

Dust and the scent of decay replaced the strongly pungent atmosphere and the torch beam, momentarily, picked out the shape of something moving away from them that was soon gone. Emma went down again, this time tripping over the broken bits from the standing stone that had straddled across the duckboards and, as Herb helped her up again, he tried to clear a path through the rubble. With her clinging to him like a limpet, and refusing to let go, this was easier said than done but he eventually managed it and even pocketed a few small pieces of rock that seemed unnaturally light in weight.

The sound of the inrush of water became louder and this, together with a grinding noise from far below, sent them scurrying back along the tunnel. The loss of electrical power had knocked out their lights, and the salvage pumps, so the pulses of the violet strobe light became their only salvation.

'Can you hear me?'

The question, initially muffled and far away, was constantly repeated as the pair approached the cage until Herb answered; 'We're both alright.'

The voice from above replied; 'I'll fetch the truck and back it up to the pit head.'

Emma had now unlatched herself from Herb and together they managed to pull away some of the timber wreckage heaped against the cage. She shone her torch inside to where the still figure of the Site Engineer, covered in dust and with his head cradled between his knees, sat on the floor with his legs askew.

'Mr Saidler!'

There was no answer so Herb moved forward and tried to kneel but his leg gave out and he only succeeded in toppling over.

'Jim!' he asked again as he struggled to his feet.

'Herbie!'

Basil's voice, clearer than before, called his name so he moved back outside the cage.

'I'm here.'

'The truck's electrics are dead.'

'Are the generators still running?'

'Yes but the switchboard's blown out.'

'There must be some sort of back up power.'

'Those cables have been melted too!'

'Jesus!'

'Are there any of the Komitoto dump trucks around?' Herb asked eventually.

'There's a couple over by the store house. Why?'

'They're inertia start diesels with no electrics.'

'Of course, they're the spring handle wind up jobs?'

'Yes, try one of them.'

'I'll see what I can do.'

'And hurry...'

A pocket of air suddenly ruptured up through the rising water level like an explosive charge filling the chamber with spray, but Emma had shifted her concern from herself to Jim Saidler, who was breathing fitfully while shivering violently in the cold and humid atmosphere.

'Hypothermia's setting in with the shock and we need to get him out of here quickly.'

Before Herb could answer the sound of a high-revving diesel filled the air and Basil's voice came through above the din.

'Is Saidler OK?'

'He's into shock and may have broken something so we'll have to lash him flat onto a board.'

'Let me lower down the winch wire first. Mind your heads!'

The grinding of gears preceded a shower of dust and rocks but eventually a large hook appeared on the end of a wire and bumped gently against the cage.

'Basil!'

'Here,' came the reply.

'The cage could be too heavy to lift out and I don't want a bloody great dump truck jammed down my escape route if you tip over!'

'I'll hoist you each up by the winch wire then.'

'We've got a big axe down here on the fire board but we need a pallet or an old door, some rope to tie him on with and a truck tyre for us.'

'Stand away from the cage, there's lots of bits around here and I'll fetch some blankets from the truck!'

It took some time but they finally had Saidler cocooned in blankets and securely lashed to a substantial wooden pallet, one of several items that Basil had tumbled down from above, and had managed to fashion a rope sling under and around the pallet and hooked it on to the wire. The dump truck slowly took the strain and the load started to rise. Every corner seemed to catch on every down facing snag of the shaft on its way up but they eventually completed the lift.

Basil then manhandled the load, with Saidler still secured, and laid it in the shade. He lowered the winch wire again and Emma, threaded uncomfortably down through the tyre but clinging on for dear life, was fendered safely from the rock faces and slowly winched to the surface. Herb's ascent was more eventful as the dumper ran out of fuel when he was half way up so he had to be lowered down again until another dumper was started to complete the lift.

They managed to carry the heavy first aid box from the office and into the shade by the truck. Emma, by this time, was utterly exhausted and literally dragging her feet from one task to another but she slowly worked herself out of the trauma by keeping busy. Every time she tried to rest the tears would flow, the violent shakes would start again, so she concentrated on the here and now instead of the then and gone.

'God! I'm glad to be out of there,' she said and dragged a crate opposite to where Herb was slumped. 'And the weightlessness I felt just seemed to multiply every effort tenfold except when I was actually lifting!'

'So it wasn't my imagination then,' he answered as Emma sat down and started to bandage his knee. 'I thought the rocks were porous or something but it must have just been the reduced gravity that made them feel lighter.'

She finished the binding and dressed various other cuts and bruises which they had all sustained. After releasing Saidler, who was conscious but unable to stand or talk coherently, from his bondage, they all sat together in the shade again to ponder their next move.

The three mobile phones were dead, the truck still wouldn't start, but they urgently needed sustenance so they ate Marie's packed lunch, together with the coffee and soft drinks, and this gave them the extra energy to carry on.

'There must have been a huge surge of magnetics,' Basil concluded after he had rummaged around the office, eventually finding the keys to the fuel tanker, and failing to start that engine either. 'Or some other force to have knocked out the mine electrics. And it's still around to disable the phone and truck circuits so we need to move out of the energy field.'

Herb picked up an empty jerry can and limped over to the diesel bowser.

'Let's load some extra fuel up on the dumper and tow the truck away from whatever's affecting it.' Basil nodded in agreement and followed Herb's example while Emma attended to Saidler who was trying to stand and moaning softly.

They had soon filled enough cans and stacked them in the dumper's shovel. Basil then attached the winch wire to the truck while Herb rigged a makeshift canvas awning to give some sort of protection from the sun. Saidler's condition had obviously worsened so he was rewrapped in blankets, lifted up onto the truck-tray, and Emma settled herself beside him hoping to prevent too much sliding around. The track out of the area was rough anyway, without the added problems of being on the end of a towline and therefore unable to avoid the potholes and slips.

When they had secured everything Basil started the dumper while Herb took the wheel of the truck and the convoy slowly moved off.

Driving along the track was a nightmare as the temperature was well into the 40s and they had to stop frequently to top up with fuel and shovel off the dust which was thrown up onto the truck's bonnet by the dumper's huge tyres. Herb had great difficulty in positioning his bad leg comfortably beside the throttle pedal, and with seeing anything out of the windscreen, but they soon settled into a stop-start routine and made reasonable progress.

Basil didn't hear the truck's horn blowing constantly, the windows being shut against the noise, but knew something was happening when the engine slowed as the load dragged. Herb had started the engine and, when he couldn't attract Basil's attention with the horn, pumped at the foot brake. They unhitched the tow wire then parked the dumper off the main track and continued their journey in the truck.

The phones were still out of range but they finally reached the tarmac highway where their mobiles picked up a signal and Herb alerted the authorities to their plight. The paramedics instructed them to carry on driving, which they did for a while, but their patient became quite agitated at the continued movement from side to side so they parked up in the shade until an ambulance eventually came over the horizon with its siren wailing and strobe light flashing.

Saidler, who had by this time lapsed into unconsciousness, was carried into the ambulance along with Basil whose every orifice was clogged solid with dust. Emma took over the driving from Herb, and followed in the truck, but it was soon flagged down by a Land Rover heading out to the mine.

Herb slid back the window, opened the door, and leaned out to bring the two company engineers up to date with the situation. They appeared sceptical when he explained about the energy force but ended up looking most uncomfortable when he refused to accompany them back to the mine.

'I don't work for Onesiphorus and I'm not covered, insurancewise that is, except if I've been contracted for specific jobs!'

'But surely in this situation…'

'I had to sign an indemnity form for my visit today and when Daniel escaped from the lion's cage he didn't go back for his bloody hat!'

The irony was lost on the pair but one of the engineers repeated the plea.

'Surely in these circumstances…'

'Your firm is one of several around here with a somewhat dubious reputation of dragging out accident insurance claims…'

'I can assure you…'

'No if's or but's. You sort it out and then call on me if needed.'

He slammed the truck door and leaned out the window; 'And if you want my advice you'll go back to town and advise Mr Big to send in the front line disaster troops before anything else!'

The truck moved off but Herb watched the engineers in the mirror for a time, scratching their heads and obviously in a quandary regarding what to do, until they were obscured by the dust clouds.

Chapter 10

Another Land Rover flagged them down before they'd driven much further and re-directed them to a local petroleum storage depot that had offered their cleaning and decontamination unit. This was gratefully accepted after which the depot's minibus shuttled them to a clinic, on the outskirts of town, for a medical examination. Two wheelchairs, with their attendants, were waiting in the car park for the patients who were now clothed in bright orange coveralls. The driver opened out the side door and waited while the chairs were manoeuvered into position.

'You're in safe hands now,' he assured them as he stood by the steps, 'so I'll be on my way.'

They thanked him before being helped down and into the chairs.

'I hope they don't think we work for this outfit.' said Emma indicating the insignia of the petroleum company on the coverall pocket before settling back as the attendant stooped to close the footstep.

'The colour suits you,' replied Herb, 'although I do miss my y-front support!'

'These paper knickers aren't so hot either. So did they really have to fumigate everything we had on?'

'The supervisor assured me that they will be returned laundered in a day or so.'

'What about my watch and ring? And the mobile phones?'

69

'Everything will be accounted for. You have my word on that.'

'I'm George Lauder, the Chief Nurse of the Unit.'

The attendants had deposited them in a comfortable lounge where one of the staff was reading the paper. He stood as they came in.

'What is this place?' asked Emma looking around.

'It's a Trauma Isolation Unit and we'd like to keep you in overnight for observation.'

'Do we have a choice?'

'You're first and foremost our guests but you've evidently experienced quite an event so we'd be grateful if you could tell us about it.'

'Sort of de-briefing before being allowed back into the outside world!'

The Chief Nurse smiled, reached for a noteboard, and sat down at the desk.

'The sooner we can download, no other word for it in this day and age, the clearer a picture you can describe. If you return to your families tonight who will definitely want to hear about the day, and then maybe describe the events later to friends over a few drinks, what you remember tomorrow could be quite different.'

'I'd like to phone my wife,' said Herb and Emma asked to contact Paul.

'Have you spoken to them since the event?'

'Only briefly on the mobile which was most unsatisfactory,' answered Herb.

'I'd prefer if you didn't for the moment but if you give me their numbers then I'll ring now and bring them up to date.'

'What's happened to Basil and how's Jim Saidler?'

'Basil is in another ward but Jim was kept in hospital for observation I believe.'

'Can we see Basil?' asked Emma.

'Not for the moment,' was the reply.

'Why not? We were all in it together.'

The Nurse checked his notes.

'Not really as you two were below ground during the event and Mr Johnson was above.'

'Why do you keep on referring to it as 'an event'?' asked Herb.

'What else can I call it,' replied the Nurse and shrugged his shoulders. 'I've been told there was an explosion at a mine and the company requires a first hand report from the people at the scene.'

'Well let's get started,' said Herb hopefully, 'and we might all get home this evening if we're lucky!'

George left the lounge and returned a little later with two young men.

'These doctors,' he said pointing to the pair, 'are dying to know what happened but they've given me their word that they will refrain from asking and concentrate on a thorough physical examination.'

He looked at them both and smiled then turned back.

'So please don't discuss it with anyone and I will see you after I've reassured your loved ones that you are in safe hands and staying overnight.'

He wrote down the phone numbers after which they were helped back into the chairs and wheeled out into the corridor.

The medical examination took an hour after which they were moved to private rooms and that was the last they saw of each other until the following evening.

In Emma's room George was waiting and handed her a menu card.

'Order what you like and if there's nothing you fancy we can send out. Onesiphorus Mining is in the chair so take this opportunity!'

She smiled although she didn't feel very hungry so she opted for an omelet with salad but then added a sticky toffee pudding just in case. A porter took her order then George sat opposite her, switched on his recorder, and opened his notepad. He tested her powers of observation, primarily, and then asked if she had slept well the night before. She admitted that she hadn't, what with the sorting of the filming gear, and he went on to enquire about any drinking, smoking, or drug taking habits.

'What on earth has that got to…'

Her answer was interrupted by a soft knock and a young man entered carrying two trays and a clipboard tucked under one arm.

'This is Dr Lawton who hasn't had his supper either so I hope you don't mind him joining you…'

The statement seemed to linger in the air as George switched off his recorder, closed his notepad and, with a friendly nod to each, left the room.

Ralph Lawton stayed with Emma until one o'clock in the morning. He had recently completed a degree in medicine from Capricornia and was halfway through a series of taster courses in various specialist fields. This enabled the new doctors to decide if they wanted to specialise in anything in particular or remain in general practice. Ralph admitted that psychiatry wasn't really his scene and he was looking forward to sampling his next taster at a Veterans Hospital in Adelaide.

They finished their meal, and he even gave Emma, who had suddenly found her appetite, his dessert. She was still hungry so he left and returned with a selection of cheeses, a pile of crackers, a melon, and the remains of a packet of chocolate covered biscuits.

When they had settled back with a second mug of coffee and Emma happily munching away on the biscuits, he switched on his recorder and flipped open his note pad.

'Tell me what happened then…'

It was after midnight before Herb's interview was completed. Every so often an orderly would appear, to check and replace the recorder tape, then hand a paper to George that listed points from the previous tape needing further clarification.

The next morning Emma and Herb spoke on the phone with their respective partners. Neither of them asked specifically what had happened and both seemed restrained, as if they had been asked not to mention the event, but it was good to hear from them. They were then served breakfast, still in isolation, before they were visited in turn.

'I can't see me staying here another 24 hours will improve my memory!'

The Chief Nurse nodded and leaned forward: 'It takes time to analyse these tapes and what we have so far is so way out that we desperately need to dot the i's and cross the t's while it's still fresh in the mind and unsullied by repetitive repeating to family, friends, and neighbours!'

'What about the financial part of it? I can't afford not to be earning.'

'Basil assures me that both you and Emma will stay on the contract rates, as if you were still filming, until this is cleared up.'

Herb thought for seconds and nodded. 'OK then but I need to use that phone...'

'Be my guest but don't forget that a story either loses or gains, something, every time it is re-told.'

'My lips are sealed in that context...'

They finally met up for supper that evening. Their written statements and voice tapes were checked, then the individual stories cross checked until George reluctantly called a halt when it became obvious that the interrogation had run its course and both the participants, and the staff, were exhausted.

Basil then joined them, he had been home since the morning, followed by Dr Lawton who came in and handed out copies of their transcripts. They compared one with the other and, apart from a few minor points, the statements were accurate regarding the sequence of events.

'I'll send in some fresh coffee while I sort these out.'

Emma said that would be good then asked the doctor about Jim Saidler.

'He's been flown out and I'm afraid that's all I know at the moment!' he replied then gathered up the statements and left the room.

Basil checked the door was shut before speaking.

'Jim Saidler's in a Psychiatric Hospital in Brisbane.'

'Like some sort of delayed shock?'

'Worse than that,' was the reply. 'He didn't seem to respond to any of the tests on his touch, sight or hearing and his body temperature kept dropping so they immersed him in a heated bath.'

'What do they think it is?' Emma asked again.

'I was over at the Cottage Hospital here talking to the Matron and she said he'd lost all feeling and emotions. Like some of the really bad shell shocked survivors from the wars was how she described it.'

He paused then added as if to clarify the statement.

'She's worked in quite a few Veterans Hospitals in her time and most of the First World War cases are well documented so these tend to be referred to especially when any present day problems with servicemen or others arises.'

They sat in silence for a while, each with their own thoughts, until Dr Lawton returned to join them.

'Can we leave this evening?' Emma asked hopefully.

'You can leave at anytime,' he replied, 'but the morning would be better.'

'Surely you've got all you want from us...'

The doctor leaned forward and picked up a biscuit before answering.

'Last night you both slept well, helped by medication, but tonight there will be no such luxury.'

'Sort of cold turkey,' added Herb.

'Why should we do this?' asked Emma.

'The voice recorders will be on as you sleep so if you think of anything else during the night, anything at all, just repeat it slowly out loud and the tapes will pick it up.'

'I'll feel a bit of a burke talking to myself,' complained Herb.

'Then jot it down on the pads but remember to push the button on the digital clocks so we can link up the time with any other nocturnal mutterings.'

'And then we can go back to the land of the living tomorrow?'

'Of course, of course.' He looked at the biscuit and then at Emma.

'May I eat this now…'

Chapter 11

He opened the passenger door and helped Emma out. Normally she would have shaken off his offered arm but the recent events had drained her energy. Paul had been up since dawn, first to see Jeff out on the early flight and then to pick up the pair at the Unit. He dropped Herb off first and then carried on back to the motel.

'It's like I've been constantly reversed these last few days, then fast forwarded, and I can't seem to distinguish between reality and fantasy.'

Emma finished speaking and turned her head away from Paul who was seated in a chair beside the bed.

'I'll make some coffee. Could you eat some scrambled eggs or toast or both?'

She shook her head then turned her face back to the wall so he sat for a while until he eventually walked through to the kitchen and switched on the kettle.

A visit to the doctor the previous day, primarily to discuss Emma's condition and probable symptoms, revealed that she would want to sleep at odd times, might possibly lose her appetite and that Paul should make sure she drank plenty of fluids. The doctor left his private and mobile number, in case of emergencies, and promised to visit in a day or two.

'We went for a walk this morning and she was much better afterwards, even more so when all the fumigated gear arrived neat and clean and complete.'

Paul was on the phone to Herb.

'I felt like ratshit for the first couple of days too but I'm OK now.'

'It's been over a week now and this was the first sign of any improvement.'

'Let's hope it continues…'

'Shall I bring Emma with me or leave her be?'

'I think she should rest, so better come over on your own and check out whatever information he has for us.'

Basil had arrived back from Brisbane the previous evening and, although he had several meetings scheduled, he wanted to see them all later that morning. This was the first they had heard from him since leaving the Trauma Unit and he initially contacted Herb, to pass the message on to Paul, who had been looking after Emma all that week with a little help from his friends, the doctor, and the practice nurse.

'I'll tell her about it and she can decide,' Paul confirmed and hung up.

His offered arm was pushed away as she stepped, quite nimbly under the circumstances, out of the car.

'Herbie thinks you should rest…'

This statement, repeated earlier, was the catalyst that had got Emma off the bed and into the shower before confronting the dressing table mirror.

'God I've lost weight and look scrawny,' was the first comment but she cheered up when the waistband on her skirt buttoned up with no effort at all.

'An ideal appetite suppressant.'

'What's that?' asked Paul.

'A day trip to one of the mines!' was the reply.

'Come in, come in and sit down!'

Three chairs had been obviously cleared of files and folders, which lay in piles on the floor, and a huge jug of steaming coffee with mugs and a carton of milk sat in a space cleared on the cluttered desk.

'Leave us please Janet and no calls or callers.'

The secretary nodded and retreated to the outer office.

'Help yourself,' said Basil indicating the tray and sat down at the desk. He opened a folder and continued. 'Now where shall I start...?'

He paused again then chose his words carefully; 'A freak occurrence, a momentary shift in one of the earth's plates causing a surge of magnetic force until Mother Nature regained control once again.'

'Is that what actually happened?' asked Paul.

'According to Onesiphorus who assures me that all is once again under control!'

'What about the filming then?'

'The company's concerned about the risk of earth subsidence around the site, and your subsequent safety, so the permission to film has been withdrawn.'

'Can they do that?'

'The leaseholders can dictate the rules and we were there by invitation.'

'There must be something...'

'I'll no doubt go up there eventually and, if they make an equipment or structural insurance claim, then I'll go up sooner to assess the damage but so far they haven't and I don't think they will.'

'What about the events at the mine then?' asked Paul.

'We all had to sign indemnity forms as it was only a social visit…'

'But surely if they start mining…'

'Ah. When they start mining. When, the operative word!'

Basil looked from one to the other and continued; 'When they actually start mining, maybe this year or next, and if they carry insurance from one of the companies I represent and I find that some safety issue has been breached, then I will have the full authority to investigate after giving the company due notice.'

'What about Jim Saidler?' asked Herb.

'I could get no information about him at all. The company has closed ranks and I was given the standard statement *'As well as can be expected'*.'

'Is anyone interested in what happened to us up there?'

'One of life's problems is that if an event does not fit into a certain category, or it can't be explained away by the powers that be, then it is tactfully ignored and relegated to the *'nearly out but not quite'* tray!'

'Will there be an inquiry?' asked Paul.

'Possibly but as no-one was killed, and there was no threat to either life or the immediate environment, then there's no urgency for any inquiry in the not too distant future.'

Basil closed the folder and stood up.

'I'm sorry that all the news is negative but a line has to be drawn under this particular project for the moment. I've got another job to look at this afternoon and I'm late already.'

'So that's it…'

'I'm afraid so,' he said and walked round from his desk to stand in front of Emma. 'I'm sorry it's ended this way but life moves on. If you need assistance to pack up and transport your filming gear then phone Janet. And don't forget to send in all your expenses, the motel bill, and the plane fare receipts, as soon as you arrive home in Brisbane.'

He looked at his watch. 'I've got to go so good luck…'

With that he walked quickly through the outer office and out the door leaving an aura of stunned silence behind at the finality of his actions.

'Take that table in the corner, I'll get a couple of jugs.'

They had ventured into the front lounge of the Criterion Hotel where Herb quickly ordered and followed them over to the table with the drinks.

'If they think they can treat us like that…'

She was stopped mid sentence by Herb banging down his glass.

'For God's sake Emma, will you put your mouth into park until I've at least had a drink. I need time to think and then we'll discuss any business outstanding!'

'Don't you dare…'

This time it was Paul's turn to interrupt.

81

'Back off Emma and let Herbie be for the moment.'

Paul could sense, after a painfully long period of silence, that the pair had things to sort out their way so he bought another jug at the bar and walked towards the Pool Room to watch an ongoing match.

'I didn't mean to snap at you but I really needed time to calm down.'

'I know, I know. It was most unexpected...'

'I've known Basil a long time and he's always been straight in all his dealings.'

'So why treat us in this way?'

'He's a bit short on the niceties in life but he usually gets his point over.'

'And what was that then?' she asked quite petulantly.

'We had a film to make. The budget and a time scale were agreed upon. The film has been cancelled, the budget spent, and we're into extra time. End of bloody story!'

'It all seems so—I don't know—so conveniently shelved.'

'I can see your point but Basil had to wrap this up now. The Trust Fund hasn't got access to the sort of funding that the Heritage Society has and no doubt the board members reminded him that they can't carry on subsidising us.'

'But what happened at the mine——surely that needs further investigation?'

'I agree but, as he said, he's got to draw a line under this particular project and to bring this particular episode to a close.'

'When you put it like that...'

'And I'm sure he doesn't want us snapping at his heels, like a couple of Jack Russells, while continuing to drain the John Cowan Memorial Fund.'

'I suppose you're right in that context.'

'So let's wrap this up, return to basics, and then see what happens.'

'Nothing else for it,' agreed Emma and emptied the dregs of the jug into Herb's glass before walking over to the bar for another.

Chapter 11

They had only been back in Brisbane a few hours when their agent phoned. A crew, working on a film documentary in the Blue Mountains, had been hit with food poisoning and replacements were needed. Emma wasn't one hundred percent fit but she agreed as the new challenge might take her mind off recent events. Paul was offered work on the same project; he was well versed in all aspects of the industry, so Saffie only had a half days respite from the Kenwood Residential Kennels before she was deposited, yet again, back on their doorstep.

Within a week the original crew had recovered and Paul was offered a few extra days so Emma returned to Brisbane alone. On her way from the airport she picked up Saffie, and the mail from the post office box, before arriving home thirsting for a proper cup of coffee so switching on the kitchen percolator was her first priority.

She walked back into the lounge flicking through the post that contained the usual flyers and adverts, bills, a cheque from Basil, and a small Jiffy Bag. Emma stripped off the seal and tipped an audiotape onto the table then shook the bag out again, expecting a note or card, but that was all.

The post-mark read Charters Towers Main Post Office, the date a week ago, and the writing printed by a black marker pen with no return name or address. The tape was the micro type, used with a standard machine, so she rummaged through her equipment bag and found the voice recorder.

'Coffee first!' said Emma and Saffie followed her through to the kitchen.

It was a woman's voice, sounding slightly muffled but quite audible; who initially apologised for using this mode of communication then went on to say that she had information about the gold mine at Native Dog Creek.

At this point Emma switched to pause then went over to her desk where she attached a lead from her master recorder into the smaller one's external speaker jack and resisted the urge to rewind as some tapes, especially those in the clandestine category, may well have been doctored to wipe after one play.

She switched on both machines then settled back in the chair with a pen and paper and her coffee.

'We apologise for the delay but Flight QF09 is now expected at 20.55 hours.'

Emma replaced the page marker and pushed the book into her pocket. She had been waiting for Paul's flight to land since seven o'clock and, apart from missing his presence in her life and work, she was desperate to share the contents of the tape with him.

The communicant hadn't given a name, or revealed how she knew about Emma or obtained her address, but stated that; *'The mine should be left at peace and the bodies contained therein left likewise.'*

The voice went on to say that the management of the mine had been transferred to a company in

Japan as Onesiphorus were quite within their rights to offload it off-shore for *Exploratory Research Purposes and Subsequent Data Evaluation.*

The mine was not yet producing so the only personnel involved at the moment were the present company's staff. However this would soon change as the new company, Mandora Pi Exploration, planned to replace them with their own workforce from Japan and the Philippines over the next few days and from then on only a few locals might be employed for mundane above ground tasks.

At some point soon the company would step deftly out of the limelight and any chance of access to the mine, or even an inquiry into the recent happenings, would be lost as the Exploratory Phase might go on for years with no, or very little, details released to the public. The woman ended by stating that she was praying that this desecration of her ancestor's last resting place would cease as she was at the end of her tether and life would never be the same again. At that point her voice broke, a minute or so of silence followed before she recovered, then she promised to keep Emma informed of any future developments.

They were sitting up in bed listening to the audiotape for the umpteenth time.

Paul leaned over to switch off the recorder and turned to Emma: 'This ancestor thing intrigues me as it indicates that a descendant, or descendants, must have survived long enough to marry and have a family, for the bloodline to have carried on. This may be what's causing her emotional distress or it could be some sort of religious fervour connected to the sect.'

'Well we know that there were some survivors so she could well be from one of their lines.'

'Maybe she's an employee of the company on some sort of fantasy trip. How old would you say she is?'

'Her formative speech pattern is 1940's. I'd say mid-late 60's'

'Yes, I'd say the same,' Paul agreed then asked; 'have you phoned Herb yet?'

'No. I wanted to hear what you thought of it.'

'Not a lot we can do apart from phoning up the newspapers and blowing the gaff on the whole scam.'

'That wouldn't do much good as there are too many loose ends floating around and the company's PR would just deny it. Basil must know some of the details but he wouldn't pass on any info to us, why should he, although Herb might well have heard something on the grapevine.'

'Onesiphorus is certainly winding up the drawbridge on this one,' Paul mused, 'but other companies or even the State Government may well be involved. Whatever we decide we must be well prepared so let's try some try other lines of inquiry first and see what comes out of the woodwork.'

'I'll second that and now can we get some sleep,' said Emma with a sigh and snuggled down into the duvet.

'I've had time to look through some files at the local historical group and Chris, the Custodian, is a whiz kid on the Internet.'

'You've no idea who this *Deep-throat* might be then?'

Paul was on the phone to Herb, a list of queries on the desk in front of him, and he wanted answers on these before starting on another tack.

'Not really,' was the reply, 'but send the tape up and I'll have a listen.'

'I'll do that now. What's this about the Local Historical Society then?'

Herb revealed that the only board members of DMMC were a couple both in their 90s and living in separate nursing homes at Bundaberg. A nephew living in the area, a Charles Clark, had power of attorney for their estate but the actual company's affairs were in the hands of Tom Epthorne.

'Chris unearthed something else as well.'

'Not more survivors surely!'

'No but you never know,' replied Herb. 'The DMMC was first re-registered a few years back as a memorial society.'

'What, remembering the disaster?'

'Yes, that together with research for which it received a grant and charitable status. Then an odd thing happened. It was de-registered as a memorial society, with the subsequent loss of its charitable status, at the end of one tax year and then immediately re-registered as a proprietary company!'

'I'll guess whose hand was on the helm during that nifty piece of footwork.'

'Tom Epthorne of course!'

'Look,' continued Herb. 'Chris is only too pleased to carry on digging for want of a better phrase.'

'Can he be trusted?' asked Paul.

'I'll handle him don't you worry. Now, have you got a pen that works?'

Herb then listed the details of the addresses and phone numbers before wishing them both well and ringing off.

'If we leave early we could easily be up and back in the same day.'

She looked over Paul's shoulder at the road map spread out on the table.

Emma had phoned the nephew during the week and his voice sounded familiar but she couldn't quite place it. He was very amicable though and they arranged to meet at the midday buffet at the *Nanking Asian Emporium*.

It was decided that she should handle the lunch date herself while Paul searched the library for any details regarding the project and the two board members, before contacting the Social Services and possibly the care homes themselves.

Paul also said he would text her after two o'clock just in case!

'Miss O'Sullivan! Emma! Over here!'

She turned from the front desk at the Emporium to acknowledge the man waving in her direction and calling her name. The place was very busy and she elbowed her way past the crowded food counter to one corner where a number of tables had been set up together.

'Hello, I'm Charles Clark. Please sit here next to me.'

The other men moved around the table to make a space for her.

'I'm sorry about the crowd, it's usually quiet midweek but Malcolm sprung a surprise birthday on me and the rest of Bundaberg seemed to follow suit.'

Emma nodded and made herself comfortable. Her host, who was good looking, dressed casually and looked in his late 30s, turned towards her. She had no problems with the gay community but it took her a few moments to gather her thoughts after being plunged, quite unexpectedly, right into the middle of a restaurant full of them.

'Have we met before?' she asked turning towards him.

'A long time back,' he replied. 'And I bet you don't remember!'

'Gotcha,' challenged Emma. 'Sydney Mardi Gras 2000.'

'How on earth…' exclaimed Charles but Emma continued; 'you dragged that awful drugged up transfuckwhit off my back, the one who was threatening my eyes with its filthy fingernails…'

She paused, realising that her table and most of the patrons on the adjoining tables had lapsed into silence listening to her tirade, so her only reprieve from an awkward situation was to play to the crowd.

'And Charles, the unassuming hero who sits quietly reserved at my right hand, rescued this poor straight media student from a fate worse than death.'

'My hero. My hero,' chanted someone on the next table who then stood up and waved an arm. 'Let's all drink to my hero.'

And with that his fellow diners stood to toast their hero who obviously enjoyed the adoration and bowed to the occasion.

'I loved the straight bit ducky. Well done, I'm very impressed,' whispered Charles after the level of conversation had returned to normal.

'Thank you,' she replied, 'but I'd like to talk to you alone.'

'Of course, but let's enjoy the food first and then we'll go for a walk.'

Chapter 12

They were strolling alongside the Botanical Gardens and Emma had just finished explaining to Charles her interest in the history of the mine. She chose not to relate any of her own experiences and tried to make her interest appear purely academic.

'I sense you are keeping something back,' he replied, 'and that's understandable in the circumstances but I really don't see how I can help.'

'What I'm looking for is any information whatsoever on the victims, on their religious background, the persecution they suffered, other church groups they may have been connected with, details on the mine itself, any letters, deeds, or news-paper cuttings appertaining to your aunt and uncle's involvement in DMMC.'

'That's quite a wide swathe of information you're asking for. Surely Tom Epthorne would help as he handles everything appertaining to the company when I only deal on a personal day to day level...'

'He's a typical accountant who will protect his client's interest and no way would he open up the files to me without a court order.'

'I don't quite follow you,' he said indicating a seat in the shade.

They both sat down and he continued; 'Surely the company's only some sort of memorial society, a charity institution that would involve the most basic type of management, and the reason the old folks were asked to join is because they were descended from the only survivors of a mining disaster back in the 1880s.'

Emma coughed, almost spluttered, into her hanky handily tucked into her cuff as she struggled to stabilise her thoughts.

'Are you alright?'

'Yes, of course,' she replied then regained her composure before asking; 'Have you any idea when the memorial society was formed or when your folks actually joined?'

'Before Christmas 95 I think, because I arrived home from the States for the New Year and the oldies were still complaining about Tom Epthorne and his wife.'

'They came up for a visit then?'

'Tom was evidently quite rude when the folks questioned all the paperwork but he then apologised and assured them it was just to clarify that they were the bone-fida descendants.'

'Do you think they knew what they were signing?'

'I suppose so but once past a certain age the older generation, most of them anyway, tend to do as they're told. Why do you ask that?'

'I don't know,' she replied. 'I haven't met Tom but my partner said he can be quite abrupt!'

They lapsed into silence for a while and then Emma asked; 'Did Tom visit again, or were any further papers sent up for your folks to sign?'

'Not to my knowledge and I'm certain they would have told me if they'd seen him recently or received anything that needed signing.'

'Look,' continued Charles looking pointedly at his

watch and getting to his feet. 'I have to go now but I'll keep what you said in mind and see what I can do to help. It's been very nice and I will be in touch.'

Emma took the outstretched hand and returned a reasonably firm shake.

'Thank you for the enjoyable lunch and the stroll. And I would sure appreciate any help you can give…'

On the return trip Emma told of her day, not so successful as she had hoped owing to the fact that it seemed to pose more questions than it answered, but Charles might well come up with something later on. And if what he said about the memorial society was true, and being registered as a charity institution if that's the right title, then that would definitely warrant further investigation on how it became a proprietary company overnight without the knowledge of its two board members.

Paul had had better luck with George, a staff member at the library with an interest in local history who not only guided him through the reference section but took him down to the basement archives that was not normally opened to the public. Although the disaster occurred some distance away from Bundaberg, the family became quite prominent townspeople and being the sole survivors of such an event only added to their prestige.

Throughout the afternoon they accessed a multitude of records, old census forms, newspaper reports and a pile of hand written reports that revealed quite a lot of background on the old couple.

'Mark Hopkins was the son of Luke and Maisie Hopkins.' Paul recounted, 'and they were the youngsters tending the livestock at the mine when the flooding occurred.'

'A coincidence that they shared the surname with the Witch Hunter or something more sinister?' asked Emma.

'I don't know but they were actually cousins with the same surname too!'

'Anyway,' Paul continued. 'Mark married Sophie but they had no children.'

'So where does Charles fit in?'

'Well Mark had two older brothers, the elder one dying during the flu epidemic of 1917, and a sister who was eight years older than Mark.'

'So which line does Charles spring from?'

'The sister, Emily, married a Charles Clark so your dining companion was their grandson and a great nephew of Mark Hopkins.'

'I need time to absorb all this,' concluded Emma, and quietly nodded off for the rest of the journey.

Saffie greeted them at the front door as if they had been away for the week. After they had all eaten and another bottle of Merlot uncorked, the genealogical charts and other information were spread out on the table.

Emma opened a note pad and listed the survivors-

Luke Hopkins aged 11 tending the goats.

Maisie Hopkins aged 13 milking the cows.

Jed Wilberforce aged 22 loading coal at the open cast pit together with a possible helper (no name or other details).'

'Let's start at 1885 when the mine was flooded...'

It was early in the morning, around July/August 1885, when it happened so the other members of the sect not on duty would have been in bed and caught by the flood unawares. The report did not appear for several months and then only three of the survivor's names were listed in the news-sheet dated February 21st 1886 and detailing the disaster. The article went on to say that the cousins were being cared for by The Little Sisters of the Poor in Townsville but nothing about Jed's welfare or the fourth survivor.

The reasons for the delay in reporting the disaster may have been that the authorities, or the press, didn't think it newsworthy, or no one reported it at the time, or the survivors stayed in the mine area for a while before raising the alarm.

The next mention was in 1895 of the marriage at Charters Towers between Luke and Maisie with a footnote saying that Jed Wilberforce, who survived the Native Dog Creek Mine disaster along with the couple, gave the bride away.

Then came the birth announcements of George in 1898, Emily in 1901, David in 1905, Mark in 1910, and then a death notice for George in 1917. The latter two were from the Bundaberg Press so they must have moved away from Charters Towers after 1905 and before 1910.

'We should be able to update this genealogical chart to the present day,' said Emma clipping the cuttings together, 'and I'll e-mail Herbie to see if he can fire up this Chris from the historical group and find out what happened to Jed Wilberforce and the other one!'

'I'll do something useful like put the kettle on then,' replied Paul.

Chapter 13

Paul continued to do something useful for the next few days when he targeted Tom Epthorne and the company by researching them from every available source. He trawled the census, even included the database at the Church of the Latter Day Saints, and ended the week with a wealth of information. A good friend of his who worked for one of the major finance companies, and always seemed to have ways and means of obtaining all sorts of sensitive information, said he might be able help but this would take a few days so Paul put his research on hold and flew to Adelaide for a short-term contract.

Emma was left to sort through the findings as it was obvious that a systematic scam had been instigated by Epthorne. He must have located the mine, read its history and saw the potential as it had been in full production until the flood and so, with modern pumping and draining methods, here was a rare opportunity to re-work a mine that very few people knew about and that hadn't been 'dug-out'. Once the elderly couple were fraudulently inveigled into becoming shareholders, or board members without their specific knowledge, then the registering of the name and forming a propriety company was merely a formality.

And their names on the Articles, being direct descendents, gave the company a cloak of authenticity and respectability.

The land, SR3318, was then somehow incorporated into the company's portfolio. The fact that the company was dormant, with a hundred or so acres of unworkable land and a few soil sample analysis reports taken from the mine tailings to support the materials handling aspect of the business totalling its only assets, was neither here nor there. A set of figures was produced to the relevant authorities at the required time, and this was its only legal requirement.

It was a golden opportunity; pardon the pun, just waiting for the right moment that eventually arrived in the shape of Gwen Fortesque and Onesiphorus Mining.

Paul phoned from the airport and Emma relayed to him the news flash as it came over Channel 9. A large area of Northern Queensland, inland from Townsville, had suffered a major power cut but the energy company was confident that services would be restored in the very near future. There was also an unconfirmed report of an explosion at a mine in the Charters Towers district but no further details were available for the moment.

'I'll catch a taxi now so try to phone Herbie,' said Paul and rang off.

'Telstra apologises for any inconvenience and normal telecommunication services will be resumed as soon as possible.

'If the phones are down up that way then the Internet must be as well,' said Emma to herself as she put down the phone then thought of her mobile.

'No service available,' read the message when she tried Herb's number so she picked up the remote and switched on the TV.

'Any news?' asked Paul as he walked through the door while shushing Saffie who had erupted in an overture of joyful barking.

'They're just rehashing what's been said; nothing new, but all the phones and video links seem to be down.'

'What do you want to do?' he asked reaching for her hand.

'I'd like to fly up tonight and find out what the hell's going on!'

'Right you are,' he agreed looking down at Saffie and shaking his head; 'What was the Kenwood Kennels number again?'

'The only option is to go to Cairns, then rent a car and drive down.'

All flights into Townsville and Charters Towers had been suspended until further notice and the couple sat at the airport discussing their next move.

'We could take our own car up if you'd only bothered to get the AC fixed!'

Paul ignored the comment and stood up. 'Let's get up to Cairns somehow and we should be able to get down to Charters in 4 or 5 hours.'

This idea was easier said than done and it was after midnight before they finally gave up the flight plan when they realised every plane going north, and even some of those going in other directions, had been commandeered either by the Military or the Government. The authorities were playing the terrorist threat card, stationing armed police at every access and exit, although they seemed to be as much in the dark regarding what they were actually dealing with as the public.

The police presence however subdued the many disgruntled passengers who had been bumped off their confirmed flights. These were given meal vouchers and rescheduled, hopefully, on later flights while arriving international passengers, those expecting a connecting flight, were ferried to the city's hotels and showered with a multitude of vouchers.

Paul and Emma saw some of their contacts from the media world, and a couple who had flown in from Cairns, but they could only tell them that the army had declared a no-go area somewhere south of Charters Towers and nothing was moving in or out. The news flashes reported that power had been restored, albeit intermittently, to most areas but an important sub-station had been burnt out and the electricity supply had had to be redirected in from Cairns.

It was one o'clock in the morning before they finally arrived and headed straight for Herb's house. The journey up by car, which had taken the remainder of that night and all the next day and evening, had been fraught with delays as they were regularly shunted off the road to allow heavy plant, mostly army equipment, a through passage. It was hot and humid but Emma knew better than to pursue the

AC card as they were both tired and an argument was the last thing they needed.

Marie was waiting; they hadn't been able to contact her but she'd expected them to turn up anyway. The police had called earlier that evening asking for Herb's help and he'd gone off with them to collect some generating equipment from the airport. She didn't know when her husband would be back but had made up two bunks in the spare room and prepared some cold meats and salad for which they were most grateful. They wanted to ask questions but she looked very tired so, when she went off to bed, they were not too far behind.

Chapter 14

They slept surprisingly well and it was during breakfast when Herb arrived; having already made two trips out to the assembly area that the army had set up a few miles from the mine. He was exhausted, only managing to snatch a few hours sleep whilst waiting in line at the airport, but he had another load scheduled to be picked up before midday.

After a shower and then, over a large plateful of bacon, eggs, tomatoes, and mushrooms, he brought them all up to date on the happenings. A similar event as before, some sort of magnetic shift or variation had occurred and so widespread that it not only affected the mine's independent supply but the nearest State Electricity power line pylons as well. This in turn affected the sub station, more than 30 kilometres away, and it happened too fast for the emergency circuit breakers at the station to operate. Thankfully the transformer gates blew out thus preventing the unbalanced surge possibly getting back to the main power stations and into the National Grid.

'What's the Army actually doing?' asked Emma.

'Nothing much at the moment except doing army things like setting up some sort of vehicle and construction plant park in a base camp this side of the mine and designating anything beyond that a no-go area. Their trucks couldn't get any further, the same trouble as we had, and a helicopter was bloody lucky to gyrate down when it lost all its electrics.'

'Were the crew hurt?' enquired Marie bringing more toast and coffee to the table.

'I think they were OK as the Signals Radar Section had monitored its flight path down and confirmed a soft landing.'

Paul took a swig of coffee and remarked; 'That's interesting.'

'What is?' asked Herb.

'That the magnetic influence hasn't affected all of the electro-magnetic waves in that area and that radar can still be transmitted.'

'But the Signals Van is set up quite a way from the mine and probably outside of its field of influence.'

'An interesting concept though,' replied Emma. 'And it could well be linked with the audio sounds I picked up.'

'It's Herbie for you.'

Marie handed the phone to Paul as he walked into the kitchen.

'I've just loaded a generator at the airport. I can pick you up in an hour and we can go out to the site. Bring your washing gear, and a change of clothes, and some sort of photo I.D. as there are road-blocks in place.'

'We'll be ready when you arrive...'

'And bring your video and audio bag as there might be some photo opportunities around the site and on the journey across...'

There was no answer when she asked Herb if he'd had any rest and, from the reflection in the rear view mirror, she could see that he had slumped sideways in the back seat and was fast asleep. She had insisted on driving and they promised to wake him well before the first roadblock. Paul sat beside her deeply engrossed in a rough draft of the present situation that someone, possibly military, had left in the truck and it made disturbing reading.

Herb shook his head and looked out the widow.

'Why have we stopped?'

'Just a sanitary stop; I won't be long,' replied Paul as he opened up the truck door and walked away into the bush.

'Feeling better?'

'Yes I am,' Herb replied, climbing out of the cab and lifting up the water can from behind the seat. It had a concave stopper, into which he poured some water, then rinsed his face and neck and dried them off on a large handkerchief.

'We're a couple of miles from the base area so you'd better let me drive.'

Emma slid over into the passenger seat, expecting Herb to climb into the driver's side, but instead she heard someone call out and a shot echoed nearby.

'Just stay where you are.'

Reflected in the wing mirror she could see three soldiers in camouflage uniforms, grouped behind Paul who had one hand clasped on his head, the other holding up his trousers, and was shuffling along towards the truck.

'Look you bloody drongos..!'

It was Herb who reached into his shirt pocket for his pass.

'Stay where you are,' ordered one of the group.

'We've got a generator on the back for Doug Lawrence; he'll have your guts for garters over this.'

At the mention of that name the rifles were lowered and the obvious leader stepped forward to inspect Herb's pass.

'Why didn't you say…?'

'You bloody twats.' Paul burst out as he reached down and pulled up his trousers.

'Sorry mate,' said one of the soldiers. 'We've just got our orders to clear the area and keep it clear.'

'The bloody no-go areas another couple of miles onwards.'

'It's been extended. The Colonel will wise you up so could you all get into the truck and move along.'

'And one of you will get his balls in a sling,' threatened Paul loudly. 'For letting off that bloody-round!',

'That's Private Rambo. He gets quite excited when he comes across a bare bum squatting by a bush way out here,' one of them answered, 'something to do with his Dad being in the Navy.'

With that the other soldiers shouldered their rifles, unsuccessfully trying to stifle their laughter, and quickly walked away into the bush.

'The bastards didn't even let me wipe.' Paul was still sounding off at the embarrassing episode as they drove into the loading bay but it was all the other two could do to stifle their own laughter at the image it conjured up.

Chapter 15

'Good to meet you, I'm Douglas Lawrence!'

He shook their hands after introductions and gestured towards the coffee urn.

'Help yourself and there's some sort of pies in the hotbox.'

Emma filled up four of the plastic cups, added the whitener and sugar as requested, and handed them around.

'I'm glad you've all come up,' he said after they had all found seats, 'I need to know what the hell we're up against.'

A corporal came in at that point and placed some paperwork on the desk; 'That's the latest dead-spot areas Colonel. Gone down about twenty percent since midnight but they seem to be on the opposite side from us.'

'Thanks Richard but don't venture any further in until the suits arrive.'

'Looks like the coffee's nearly out Sir. I'll get a fresh flask sent over.'

'We're waiting for some anti radiation suits to arrive from Canberra,' he informed the group after the corporal had left and shut the mobile office door. 'They're the latest American equipment being flown in from Hawaii.'

He looked down then slid some sheets of paper towards them.

'Just write your full names and sign underneath. It's just a cover of the official secrets act, which I'm sure you are all conversant with, so your signature is required by the powers that be.'

When they had all signed he took the papers back and handed another sheet each to Paul and Emma.

'Fill these out with your details and IRD number then hand them back. The Defence Department will put you on a daily casual rate of G/3 Clerk and you're listed as Administration Assistants, for want of a better title, but you'll be well covered insurance-wise.'

He stood and walked towards the door.

'If you'll follow me I'll take you to the QM tent. You can draw coveralls and whatever else you need and Richard will find you somewhere to bunk down.'

'Any questions?'

No one spoke so he continued; 'When you've sorted yourself out, and had something to eat and drink, come back here and we'll talk. I believe that you've experienced whatever and we need help!"

Still no one spoke so he opened the door and stood aside as they all filed out.

'The Army standard of cooking has risen substantially in my eyes.'

Emma speared the last remaining piece of honey-glazed ham on to her plate and added the last tomato. They were finishing lunch in the NCOs meal tent and the three of them had enjoyed the salad buffet.

'It's all done at the Army Base in Townsville and flown fresh up here this morning,' said Herb selecting an apple from the bowl and opening up his knife.

'They seem to have got themselves sorted pretty quickly,' replied Paul.

'They learnt a lot from the Darwin episode and regular exercises, for civil emergencies that happen quite often in places like the Solomon Islands, are high on their training schedules so the administration machinery now runs smoothly.'

'Did you know we were going to be shanghaied like this?'

'Not really but, as you came all the way up for a nose-around, I can't see you have any reason to complain.'

'They could have at least asked us…'

Herb tried not to smile at Emma's indignation.

'Would you have said yes to being on a good daily rate, bed and board supplied, and another possible crack at Onesiphorus?'

'Yes but…'

'Well it's saved the Colonel the bloody trouble of asking you then…'

'Can't you get all this information from the company?'

They had been sitting in the office, answering the Colonel's questions for the last hour with a Lieutenant from the Engineers present and taking notes.

Emma's throat was sore from talking and she was enquiring why the Army couldn't get the answers they needed from Onesiphorus.

Doug Lawrence let out an extenuated sigh of frustration.

'We, or they, seem to have some sort of communication problem. The mine management was transferred to a Japanese company a month or so back.'

'What about the company engineers who were here, they know the layout.'

'They all seem to be incommunicado in Java, or somewhere, but the company assures us they are trying their best to contact them.'

'What about the Japanese, or the others that replaced them?'

'That's one of the main problems. We don't know how many, if any, people were actually on site and there's no sign of life from the limited aerial information we have so far. The satellites might give us more but all this takes time…'

'What about the power lines that caused the problems in the first place?'

'State Electricity has disconnected at the sub-station but no way are they going to venture further at the moment.'

'And I don't blame them!' commented Emma and that statement brought the meeting to a close.

'I'm sorry, I just can't allow that at the moment.'

They were into their third day on site and all Emma and Paul had done connected to the project was to try on the anti-radiation suits. These turned out to be hot, bulky and most uncomfortable to wear.

'Just to take a look around the outer perimeter is all I ask. To see if anything has changed or shifted out of place. We need to do it soon as a prelude to the main event whenever that happens so we're prepared!'

She was trying to keep the frustration out of her voice as, although the Signals detachment continued to decrease the exclusion zone, the Colonel still wanted the satellite pictures, and their analysis, before making a move.

'Bit pointless us being here then,' exclaimed Emma petulantly. 'There's so...'

The Colonel interrupted with a loud sigh of exasperation. 'Your choice but don't expect to be allowed back in the foreseeable...'

He paused, shuffled some papers, and then continued. 'Maybe it would be a good idea if you all went and then we...'

'I didn't mean it to be an ultimatum but...'

She stiffened as she spoke and then wavered; 'I didn't mean it to sound like that, it's this damn waiting.'

'Look Emma! I've got far more important things to do than argue the toss with you but you must understand the area is under Army control. If you can't hack it then go but if you stay then take advantage of the limited facilities we have here and try to be patient.'

The interview was obviously at an end as the Colonel reached for his hat.

'Yes of course. I'm sorry...' And with that she backed out of the room, somewhat shamefaced, watched by the Colonel every step of the way.

Herb had been away for a couple of days, as a contract for further runs to the airport was in the offing, and he'd gone to Brisbane to look at some additional trucks. He offered to check on Saffie, and to pick up the mail or any personal supplies required, and it was on the third day that the satellite pictures arrived at some unearthly hour of the morning. The helicopter hovered high overhead for sometime, waking the camp in the process, although it eventually had to land some distance away for safety reasons.

'What's this part here then? It seems to be teeming with some sort of life form and could possibly have an energy source there.'

'That's the swamp area,' replied Emma. 'I got a lot of audio chatter when I was there before.'

The pictures were laid out on the table, having been blown up to super-size, and the various shades indicated where the infrared beams had reacted.

An Environmental Engineer named Oscar Mantel, who had been working with the Department on unstable explosives and chemicals and other equipment that had been dumped down various disused mineshafts after WW2, had accompanied the pictures on the chopper and the Colonel had cleared it with the authorities for him to remain on site for a while.

Oscar pulled up a stool, fired up his laptop, and asked the others to stand behind him. He seemed quite conversant with the area and brought up 3-D images indicating the magnetic fault lines. These, he said, had originally run north to south but he then pointed out a section that had twisted almost to an east/west direction.

'I haven't a clue what caused it,' he admitted pushing his seat back. 'The magnetic abnormalities in this part are well documented but an acute shift like this is a one-off!'

'Any idea when this took place?' asked Paul.

'I didn't really have time to check although I did a random hit of 6 months back and there was no indication then. I'll be able to narrow it down but it'll take time.'

'What will be the effects of these shifts then?' said the Colonel.

'The earth switches its magnetic poles every 7,000 years or so; this has been proved by core samples taken at the Ice Caps, and it's obvious it's not anything that dramatic as the whole planet would be affected. However I shouldn't think that such a small shift would have much effect overall and, in time, the strongest magnetic effect of north/south, will prevail in the dislodged bit and it'll slip back into line. But I'd like to know what caused it.'

'Do you think it's safe to go in?' continued the Colonel.

'If you've the choice, no!' Oscar paused and looked around before asking; 'Has anyone heard about the Philadelphia Navy incident during the War?'

No one answered as it was obvious who had the floor; 'The US Navy was supposed to have made a destroyer disappear only to reappear elsewhere. Einstein was supposed to have been involved somewhere along the line, as he was working for the US Government at the time, but then rapidly disassociated himself from the project when it all went bottoms up!'

'What's your point then?' asked the Lieutenant. 'Do you think we have a similar situation here?'

'You asked me if I thought it was safe to go in now. All I'm saying is that huge magnetic forces were artificially generated to shift the target during the destroyer example, not dissimilar to what has naturally taken place here so, if you fancy ending up in Disney Land, then...'

This last statement should have caused some spark of amusement but the group lapsed into a strained silence as they contemplated his words.

After a few moments the Colonel got to his feet and picked up his notebook.

'Right,' he said, 'we have to do something so let's examine our options and then we'll stop for breakfast...'

These came fast and furious and, after 20 minutes or so, they had agreed on a set of procedures to follow while another meeting, for all the personnel, was arranged for later that afternoon.

Chapter 16

'Just nod and go along with what you've been told.'

This was Paul's advice to Emma as they sat in the Mess Tent with their coffee. Copies of the pictures were set out in front of them and they were identifying the paths that they could remember and labelling specific areas of the mine complex.

'These have never come from any satellites,' Emma had commented before adding. 'And I didn't think the US Spy Planes were allowed to overfly this part of the world anymore.'

'What…' she continued noticing the head shake from Paul.

'I don't care a stuff where the pictures came from,' he replied. 'All I know is that I'd prefer to work with them than not!'

The afternoon meeting was held in the canteen and they were sitting around listening to the Colonel above the noise of the fans.

'If you can't hear me either wave or sit closer,' he said leaning against the edge of the table.

'You will have noticed the Signals truck parked a couple of hundred metres down the track. The guys there have rigged part of this as a Sat Scan booster station outside of the mines influence which, incidentally, has reduced considerably since yesterday. You can now actually pick up a signal on your mobile phones so please limit your calls to five minutes. And I'd appreciate if you can use the assorted chargers set up in the truck as I'm always tripping over the ones hanging out of every bloody socket around here!'

There was a ripple of laughter and he continued; 'Things in the outside world, thankfully, seem to be returning to normal and I'd like to keep it that way. We have a 10-mile radius exclusion zone and a 20,000 feet no-fly zone in place and the various authorities are maintaining these. However, as expected, the media has a great interest in this so when you phone home be on your guard. I'm not going to labour too fine a point but please remember that we're on a military exercise here. And that's all your family and friends need to know. If any of the media gets hold of anything that could only have come from within, then I will seek out the offender and act accordingly.'

The subdued laughter immediately ceased when he added; 'And I kid you not!'

The Colonel stood up, stretched, and sat down again.

'We need to sort this out quickly but, until we know exactly what we're up against, let's leave it to the Signals and the Engineers to secure our safety.'

He stood and stamped his feet, a sure indication that the meeting was over.

'Thank you for your attention. I'll let you know of any further developments and Oscar; I'd like a word with you in my office.'

A transport chopper arrived from RAAF Townsville just after supper with, amongst its other cargo, a set of weather balloons together with a helium gas plant. The Signals Detachment already had a large truck mounted winch and the plan was to monitor how far the mine's influence extended upwards. From various positions around the site, taking into consideration the direction and strength of the wind at the time, sets of reading could be tabulated and assessed.

The mining company continued with their example of non-cooperation and legal moves against them were already being considered, (under the Public Safety Act), to produce information on any personnel thought to have been on the site and any relevant information regarding health and safety issues when entering the complex. Until then however an aerial photo-reconnaissance unit would take close up shots from above, when a certain vertical ceiling was deemed safe for local conditions, and this would assist the initial foray into the mine by the soldiers.

'The unusual aspect of this case appeals to me and it's interesting,' was his reply earlier in the day to Emma's request for information. 'And if you need my help again then ask sooner rather than later!'

Oscar was leaving on a late flight as he was involved in several ongoing projects for Defence but he had promised Emma that he'd try and pinpoint the dates of the shifts and contact her in the event of any further abnormalities.

The Colonel drove him to the flight assembly area

that evening and thanked him for his help. They shook hands after which Oscar walked towards the chopper, slung his bag up through the hatch, and climbed up the access ladder.

A couple of days later Herb had been scheduled to pick up some boxes of electrical spares from Townsville Airport but when he arrived they were still held up in the Customs Hall waiting for clearance by the agent. The accompanying paperwork was incomplete but the shipment was important to the Signal Section so he was instructed to book into a local motel and await further instructions on his mobile. It was midday and he was walking down towards the City Centre, for lunch, when someone hailed him from the other side of the road.

'Just the man I wanted, I was on my way up…'

'I'm going for something to eat and a beer so feel free to tag along.'

I'd love to,' Oscar replied then crossed over and fell into step beside him.

They avoided the 'Healthy Options' and each eventually let out a satisfied grunt.

'Let's move over to the corner table with the striped brolly, I'll get a top-up!'

Oscar returned with another jug before filling up both glasses, setting up his dictaphone and a notebook and pens, and finally looking around to satisfy himself that they were truly alone.

'Is money on the agenda?' enquired Herb grinning. 'I've promised Emma that I won't sell the story without her OK!'

'Nothing like that although this could well become too hot to handle in the wrong, or even the right, hands!'

'I'm all ears,' replied Herb and leant back in the chair.

Oscar switched on the tape, unscrewed the top off of his pen, and asked; 'One of you mentioned a descendant from one of the original survivors.'

'Yes, that was Charles Clarke who Emma and Paul went up to Bundaberg to see and she had lunch with him I think.'

'Do you have a contact number for him?'

'Not with me but I'll text it to you when I get back to the mine.'

'Remember those rock fragments you asked me to analyse, the ones you picked up down the mine during your first visit?'

'That wasn't the first visit as I'd been there a few times during the film shoot.'

'Oh…'

'And I was also Emma's driver for recording some silent film sound-bites.'

'That's right, I remember now. Nothing unusual happened then?'

'Not really apart from the weird audio readings the machine was picking up.'

'What sounds do you mean?'

'Sounds outside of our hearing range and the graph…'

Oscar interrupted; 'Why do you say that?'

'Well Saffie could hear them and the dog was doing her nut but, as I said, it was outside the normal human range.'

'Did you observe the audio readings yourself on that occasion?'

'Yes, I was following her around the site…'

'Has Emma still got the recordings?'

'Of course, that was the catalyst that started all this…'

Herb paused as he noticed the blue message light flashing on his mobile.

'The load is ready,' he said on accessing the message. 'I've got to go!'

'Shit!' Oscar slumped back and clicked the tape off.

'Sorry about that…'

'Not your fault. I've got to reassess this whole situation and go over it step by step with all of you,' countered Oscar screwing the top back on his pen and packing up his recorder. 'Let me sort something out and I'll text you…'

On his way back to the motel, Herb pondered what the rock fragments had actually revealed as Oscar hadn't quite got around to telling him.'

Chapter 17

Herb switched off the lights, then the engine, and got down from the cab. 'Here are your Spares Unclassified,' he said and handed the keys to the MT Sergeant. 'The invoices are in the glove box pinned to the Custom clearances.'

The trip down from Townsville had taken less time than expected, the roads were reasonably clear and he'd even collected some clean working gear from home, but it was tiring and he stretched and yawned as he walked along the track towards the mine. Suddenly the sounds of early evening were disturbed by the drone of a chopper, somewhere in the middle distance, that slowly became louder. It was coming in from a sun very low on the horizon then turned and commenced a slow descent over the mine. The bright colours on the fuselage, of royal blue and white vertical stripes illuminated by the perimeter lights, identified it as belonging to one of the premier media networks. But it had obviously ignored the no-fly zone believing that a front page exclusive with pictures was well worth the risk of a fine that the Air Ministry might impose for breaking regulations.

However its descent carried on as it gyrated down to earth and landed with a bang just inside the perimeter fence on the edge of the swamp.

Emma and the other two never got to see the video. The Colonel viewed it privately the next morning after which it was airlifted to Townsville, along with the Signal Officer, and followed by the rest of his section later in the day.

Herb saw most of the event from a distance, starting with the plume of dust arising as the rotor section broke away from the fuselage on impact, but when he reached the fence line there was no sign of any aircraft debris whatsoever. The surface of the swamp was as calm and unruffled as before without the slightest shred of evidence that anything unforetold had ever occurred.

However someone much closer to the event had a grandstand view and kept his head throughout. The Signal Corporal was around, taking video half light publicity shots of his section working with the various detecting equipment, when the drama unfolded, but unfortunately his view of events was partially obscured by the detached rotor gearbox and the broken blades. However someone much closer to the event had a better view and kept his head throughout. Michael McGinnis, one of the section on duty nearby, observed it all and Herb quickly surmised this fact when he arrived at the scene. Admittedly it was over and done with quickly but in those vital couple of minutes this particular soldier wasn't mesmerized and rooted to the spot like the rest of the section.

And Mike McGinnis was the man on whom Herb concentrated his efforts for the rest of that evening before he was whisked away!

It was Herb's nature to stand aside from his fellow man but, if the need arose, he could quickly adapt to the present company. And on this occasion he was convinced that immediate action was required as he knew, from past experience, that the Army always acted quickly in situations of this nature.

Emma and Paul also realised, from the frantic activity of the previous evening which continued well into the night, that an incident, or accident, involving an aircraft had taken place. But their obvious exclusion from any of the meetings with the officers left them somewhat out on a limb so they kept to themselves in their tent and played cards while sharing a couple of bottles of wine. The canteen itself however was a hive of activity with the noise increasing to such a level that the Colonel threatened to close the bar if they didn't quieten it down.

He had a hangover supreme the next morning, that much was obvious, when they found him sitting in the corner of the canteen gulping a handful of aspirins washed down with a beaker of black coffee.

'How did it go then mate?' asked Paul uncertain of what actually went where.

Herb's eyes were dreadfully bloodshot and Emma was going to suggest that he shut them before he bled to death but thought better of it.

He looked around before picking up his coffee. 'There are a few bods within listening distance so grab yourself a cuppa and I'll be under the tree stand.'

They had all settled down in the shade and waited until Herb's coughing spell subsided before any one spoke.

'Well?' asked Emma.

'Jesus, what a night…'

'Well?' Emma repeated.

'Well,' Herb started. 'You would know that something, previously airborne, came down inside the perimeter fence.'

Emma nodded.

'It was a chopper from the TV Station that crashed, or crash landed, when it lost power over the site.'

'We knew something had happened when we heard the noise and rushed out but one of the soldiers told us to stay away so it wasn't until much later that we went down for a look.'

'It all happened so fast and was over just as quickly,' said Herb drinking more of his coffee.

'When we got there the guards wouldn't let us too near but we couldn't see any wreckage or debris at all.'

'It all happened so fast…'

'What happened so bloody fast?' exclaimed Paul his voice verging on frustration as Herb struggled upright and took another swig of his coffee.

'One person saw the Full Monty but the others, including the corporal shooting the video and the rest of the squad, only saw odds and sods.'

Emma and Paul looked at each other with concern as this was an unknown facet of Herb, who seemed almost traumatized by the events, as well as being badly hung-over and on the point of incoherent rambling.

'That one person was Signalman McGinnis and Michael was my drinking buddy last night before the Army got to him.'

Herb was interrupted by the sound of an incoming flight, one of the larger troop carrying choppers and he scrambled to his feet.

'Stay a moment, I'll be back,' he said and walked quickly away.

After 15 minutes or so they got tired of waiting and walked over to the Compound wondering what had happened to him. He wasn't in the Mess Tent so they tried the Stores Tent, where he was bunked down with a couple of the other drivers, and they found him working furiously on his laptop.

'Give me another 10 minutes,' he said looking up with an expression akin to desperation, 'and I'll be through. Please. It's vital that I get this down.'

They knew him well enough not to question his reasons so they returned to the shady spot beneath the tree stand. After a while he appeared, looking even more washed out, but grinned as he sensed their looks of concern then remarked; 'I'm too old for this bloody game and thank God I'm off duty until this evening!'

As he sat down he dipped into his bush jacket pocket to retrieve two discs and handed them to Emma; 'Keep one each, in a safe place, and forget where they came from.'

'What are they,' she asked.

'One thing I learnt from our foray into the Psych Unit is that a story changes, sometimes quite dramatically, each time it's told or as each day passes.'

They waited, expectantly, for him to continue but he appeared to lose the thread of what he was saying and his shoulders slumped forward.

'What is this then,' she repeated turning the discs over in her hands.

He looked down and then, shaking his head, gazed up with concern.

'It's my report of the crash and its aftermath, as witnessed by Signalman Mike McGinnis and recounted to yours truly during a demanding night on the piss!'

Emma returned his gaze; 'Aren't you being a bit dramatic?'

'Have you seen any of the Signal bods?' he interrupted with something akin to a snarl. 'The Engineers are on picket duty as the whole bloody Signal Section was flown out on that last chopper!'

He got up and brushed the dust off of his shorts.

'So, the next time you tap your foot and hum along with; 'Once a Jolly Swagman camped by a billabong', spare a thought for Sour Waters at Native Dog Creek. And then, if you try it for real don't, under any circumstances, camp too bloody close to the edge!'

He looked from one to the other and smiled: 'Just a bit of home spun philosophy. Keep the disc safe and don't mention them to anyone.'

With that he left them to it and walked over towards the tents.

Chapter 18

'What do we call you then?'

Emma was standing beside the Lieutenant of Engineers, with whom she hadn't had a lot of verbal contact, in the Mess Tent.

'Lieutenant will do.'

'What about Loot?'

'Whatever!' he replied rather primly and then the Colonel suddenly appeared at the tent flap and addressed them; 'My office. Bring your coffees...'

Paul was about to pour his second cup so Emma quickly topped up hers and together they walked to the office.

The previous day had passed without any request for help or assistance from the Military at all. Emma's offers were abruptly turned down so they spent the free time lazing and reading and catching up on their mail. Herb was busy with the stores section in the afternoon after which he accompanied the army driver of a road tanker to load fuel at the Depot and they hadn't seen him since.

'I hate to remind you,' he started off after they had all settled down, 'but at this time more than ever I need to reinforce it.' Loot appeared puzzled by the statement so the Colonel hurriedly added; 'The Official Secrets Act of course!'

He looked around and continued; 'The Signal Section has returned to their unit and a replacement squad should be here soon. The explanation given to the media, and to the general public of course, regarding the crash could be that the helicopter simply disappeared on a routine flight and the search for it is continuing. The Army doesn't like untruths, no one does, but the bloody thing shouldn't have been anywhere in the area and in this situation it's difficult to know what's for the best!'

They listened in silence and, when he paused fully expecting a question or comment, he was surprised that there were none so he continued; 'However considering what we are trying to do here, and possibly contain, I don't want any more media attention focused on us than there is already.'

Emma indicated then asked; 'We've heard so many conflicting stories. What actually happened then?' She was going to add that the eye witnesses to the event had been conveniently whisked away but the pressure of Paul's foot against hers made her heed his warning.

'Unfortunately the chopper lost power,' replied the Colonel, 'and came down inside the fence line near the edge of the swamp and tipped over. I don't know if the movement of the people inside contributed but it became unstable and...'

'What happened to the people inside?'

He let out a sigh of exasperation and the pressure of Paul's foot increased.

'You're an intelligent woman Ms O'Sullivan, it was all over in a couple of minutes and no one had a chance to do anything so what do you think happened?'

Paul interrupted at this stage, pre-empting any escalation of Emma's views on the subject; 'I assume the bodies will be recovered, together with the fuselage, once we have access to the mine area?'

'I should think so.' he answered then stood up and closed his notepad. 'Positive things may be happening at last and I'd like to be out of here by the weekend so any more questions before we disperse?'

A plan of procedure had been worked out and after lunch, when the danger zone should have retreated well inside the fence line, the officer plus the sergeant and two armed escorts, would don anti radiation suits and venture through the main gate. Once this area was secured they would continue to scan the roadway, in grid pattern formation, right up to the mine head and beyond.

The Colonel's orders were quite specific. Emma and Paul were allowed as far as the main gate where they sat under a canvas lean-to ready to answer any queries from the advance party. Loot, as Emma had now christened him and who turned out to have a rather dry sense of humour, only had one question about the mine entrance so they enlightened him quickly then carried on with their card game and drank copious cans of coke.

They had finally accepted the Army's way of doing things and, anyway, their bank accounts had never looked healthier!

It wasn't until the following lunchtime that the whole of the above ground area was deemed safe. A

Signal Corporal with two men had arrived on the morning flight, and soon had the CCTV cameras installed at various locations where they were closely monitored from an observation truck, while the Engineers had cordoned off the swamp area and installed an electric fence. Wandering pickets patrolled over the 24-hour period but the night passed peacefully enough.

The advance party went in after lunch and secured the buildings with no major problems. Of the Japanese Site Personnel there was absolutely no sign although several half consumed meals, one even had the fork impaled upright into a steak, were still on the table in the eating area. Loot likened it to 'The Marie Celeste' mystery where the crew had all seemed to have vaporised during supper.

Some of the refrigerators had been tipped over with the ground shocks, spilling their contents onto the floor, while the food in the other units that had remained upright was found to be badly affected by the failure of the power. The flies, insects, and various vermin had had a field day, descending on the spoils in great numbers, and the soldiers were kept busy clearing up and spraying the area.

'We'll be told when we're needed.'

Paul had only just answered Emma's query when Loot appeared to relay the Colonel's message that the area had been deemed safe, and an initial survey of the top of the mineshaft was planned, so could they be on hand to assist.

As they were walking towards the mine, having changed out of their casual gear and now resplendent in green drab army overalls, hardhats and boots, one of the soldiers came out of the Stores Tent carrying Herb's rucksack together with his distinctive orange sleeping bag roll.

'Just following the sergeant's orders Miss,' he replied to Emma's query and carried on walking towards the offices.

'Why have they collected Herb's gear Loot?' asked a puzzled Emma when they met the officer at the mineshaft.

'I believe he's taking a break.'

'He was only going to the Fuel Depot the night before last. If he was leaving why didn't he come back and pack his own gear?'

'I really don't know so now can we now concentrate on the job in hand...'

'I'm still getting that audio chatter.'

Paul and the Signal Corporal were checking the back area while Emma and Loot were sitting on a bench outside the mine entrance. She pointed out the changes to the various structures and buildings that were apparent since her last visit and Loot remarked, what with all the new equipment, machinery in packing cases and various containers all parked up nearby, it was obviously the Company's intention to reopen and to rework the mine in the not-too-distant future.

As they moved and stood just inside the entrance, the buzzer sounded on her audiometer and she moved the instrument, hanging around her neck, towards Loot so he could see the violent oscillations.

'You've had these readings before though haven't you?'

'Yes but not here, just around the swamp and adjoining areas although these new signals seem so much stronger.'

'But I can't hear anything!'

'I know,' replied Emma patiently. 'They're out of our audio range.'

'Are you sure this is audio we're registering?'

'Of course! On my first visit, a few months back, my dog Saffie became very distressed at this entrance around here and couldn't wait to get out of the place.'

They backed off and sat on a sleeper slab where Loot took off his hat, scratched his head, and remarked; 'Being an officer I'm expected to lead from the front, bluster my way in exploring the terrain and slashing with my trusty sword this way and that but…'

He looked at Emma ruefully who smiled and asked; 'But what?'

'I don't feel out of my depth but…'

'But what?'

'We'll go back and see the Colonel. Maybe if we approach this from a slightly different direction it'll be safer for all concerned.'

'You go and see him and I'll try and tabulate some readings. One of the signal guys can come with me to check for any low level radioactivity and keep an eye on me at the same time.'

'OK then but don't wander off!'

Emma moved back inside the entrance where it was much cooler and waited for her escort to arrive. She was under strict orders and, as she sat, her thoughts wandered back to the first accident and how lucky they had all been to escape comparatively unscathed. She had heard nothing about how Jim Saidler was doing and...'

'Miss O'Sullivan!'

A soldier calling from the gate interrupted her thoughts and, as she stood up, she was surprised how easy it was so she promptly sat back down again.

'How odd,' she said to herself, 'that took no effort at all!'

It wasn't until she sprung up again, no other word for it, that she realised the lightness she felt stemmed from the sensation of weightlessness she had earlier experienced during the first accident one level down in the mine.

She picked up a small rock and tossed it casually towards the fence.

'Bloody Oaf Miss, you should be playing for Australia!'

The reason for this comment was that the rock had travelled far higher and much further than expected from Emma's effort.

They were all sitting in silence drinking their coffee.

Emma and her escort had immediately aborted their mission and Emma reported back to the Colonel who was having his afternoon break.

He leant forward with his head in his hands then looked up.

'I seem to have run out of options. What else can we do without putting people's lives at risk?'

He took a swig of coffee and looked at Emma. 'With this fall in gravity around the pithead I can't have anyone floating away up to God knows where!'

'Surely the mining sector has had this problem before?' suggested Emma. 'What about the magnetic abnormalities in WA and the Northern Territories?'

The Colonel drained his mug and stood up; 'I'll go over to Townsville this evening and rattle a few dags. It's been suggested that we approach this problem from a different angle and this gravity thing has convinced me that we need a few of the boffins up here. Let them sit and ponder solutions with their graphs and calculations as I'm not placing my delicate neck on the block!'

With that he motioned to Loot and they left together.

Chapter 19

Oscar arrived on the evening flight, accompanied by piles of paperwork, plus a few sophisticated measuring instruments of his own, and the Colonel was in two minds whether to stay but he stuck to his original plan and designated Loot to command in his absence. After the chopper had departed it was decided, as the hour was late and as everyone had had a long and tiring day, that they should all get a good nights sleep and start afresh in the morning.

By the time Emma and Paul had finished breakfast and walked over to the office, Oscar had drawings and photos spread over every work surface. Loot appeared, carrying a folding table, and told Paul that there was a fax from Brisbane, which had come through that morning, waiting for him in the Signal Truck.

'I'll go and see what it's about,' he replied and pulled up a chair for Emma before leaving.

'His mother's been taken to hospital,' said Loot looking at Emma. 'There's a stores flight due shortly so he can go out on that.'

'Why on earth didn't you tell him then?' asked Emma.

'Messages like that are best read in private, gives one time to gather one's thoughts and resources!'

She felt slightly ashamed at her quick retort but any apologies were cut short by Paul coming back through the door.

Emma helped him pack and the Signal Corporal brought news that a scheduled flight to Brisbane was being held in Townsville awaiting his arrival. They were both very impressed by how fast the Army could move when it put its mind to it.

Back in the office, after seeing Paul off at the helipad, she managed to put thoughts of him to one side and focus on the job in hand.

'These are the latest satellite pictures,' said Oscar spreading them out and cluttering the desktop even more, 'and my laptop shows how much the chunk of rock, that had originally shifted out of alignment, has moved back towards the north/south line.'

Emma peered at the screen. 'About ten degrees.'

'Less than that and I expected it…'

He paused and looked around. 'Where's Herbie?'

'They sent him back to base as surplus to requirements,' replied Emma.

Oscar swiftly glanced up at Loot. 'Is this true?'

'The Colonel's decision,' came the reply, 'nothing to do with me!'

'I need him back here. A lot of my theory hinges on what happened down the mine that first time with those quartz figures and I need it first hand.'

'I was there as well,' said Emma somewhat petulantly.

'Did you see the aftermath of the explosion?'

'Well no but…'

'I need Herb here then.'

Emma eyes flared; 'What I was going to say was that a very detailed report of the incident is in the files at that clinic.'

'Yes my dear,' replied Oscar somewhat condescendingly. 'But they won't give me a copy.'

'Surely the Army can get one,' suggested Loot.

'You can try, but I need either the report or Herbie, preferably the latter, before I even put my boots back on!'

It was lunchtime before Loot had any news; 'A crate is waiting to be picked up at the airport so one of the drivers, he's due some leave anyway, can pick up Herb on the way down who can then bring the load back here.'

'What about the report?' asked Emma.

'I couldn't get hold of the Colonel so I phoned a mate of mine who said that a court order was being enforced on the mining company to hand over certain documents but the report, unfortunately, wasn't on the first list so they have to make out another order.'

'God,' exclaimed Oscar. 'What sort of drongo company are we dealing with?'

'Not a very good one believe me,' replied Emma and left it at that.

He stepped down from the truck, shouldered his bag and handed the invoices over to the Duty Sergeant.

'Same bed space?' he asked.

The sergeant nodded and Herb made his way towards the stores tent where he put down his bag then laid out his sleeping bag onto the rubber mattress.

As he extended a couple of canvas stools and sat down to take off his boots, the flap of the tent opened up and Loot peered in.

'Herbie. Good to see you!'

He looked up in surprise at being greeted like a close friend, as the Lieutenant had always been somewhat standoffish towards him.

'I wanted to have a word with you before…'

'I thought there was something behind your friendly greeting!'

Loot grinned and sat down on the other stool.

'Before the rest, was what I wanted to say!'

'Go ahead then.'

'I think we need to lay the groundwork so to speak.'

'That's fine with me.'

'I'm in command here and, to tell you the truth, I feel a bit out of my depth.'

He paused then continued; 'Not as far as the military aspect you understand because it's merely a textbook case of overseeing a small detached unit.'

'The problem is the mine then and what lies beneath and within?'

'Precisely but please be assured that I want this problem solved quickly as much as you do.'

'Seeing as we're being forthright and straight,' replied Herb changing the subject slightly. 'What do you know about that last chopper crash by the swamp?'

'To be honest not a lot. I heard that the surface was somehow disturbed and possibly washed the fuselage, together with the people on board, into the swamp and I knew that one of the Signal bods had a video camera going at the time.'

He shifted to a more comfortable position and continued; 'But the Colonel didn't confide in me. I wasn't particular friendly with the Signal Officer either who seemed rather a nerd and totally immersed in himself and his own section!'

'If you didn't see the video then you must have heard the talk in the canteen that night and why was the Signal Unit shipped out so fast?'

'The unit was maybe needed elsewhere as they were a specialised one with quite a lot on. And I didn't see the video, although I've heard numerous stories from my lot that all seemed so bloody far fetched, so I decided to wait for the official report to come out before forming an opinion.'

Herb found himself warming to Loot who appeared to be a straight talking individual but who was still Army.

'So what do you suggest regarding this little project?' he asked.

'Well.' said Loot. 'You and the others give me an overview of your plans each day, together with what went on the previous day and then, if anyone important asks as I'm sure they will, I can bring them up to date on our progress.'

Herb nodded and added; 'or disasters as the case may be!'

'I'm fully aware of that fact too believe me,' he answered, 'and if I have any queries, or I see anything contravening Queen's Regulations, then we'll get it sorted before you start the day.'

Herb nodded again.

'And if you need Army assistance then all you have to do is ask.'

They both got to their feet at the same time.

'Thanks Lieutenant,' ventured Herb. 'Now let's get some of that tucker as I'm bloody famished!'

'Did you have any explanation why you were suddenly, for want of a better word, dropped?' Emma's query came after supper when Herb had suddenly joined them.

'Obviously because I was privy to what really happened to the chopper by the swamp so, by taking me out of the frame for the moment and accessing any illicitly obtained verbal evidence on my person or, in this case, on my laptop, the Army then had time to concoct a story acceptable for public consumption.'

'The Colonel seemed an OK guy though.'

'He is,' answered Herb, 'but he's still Army and has to protect his own butt.'

They were sitting away from the main buildings sharing a pitcher of iced tea.

'What did actually happen then?' asked Emma.

'My private report is on the disc I gave you and, incidentally, the file of which had been wiped off my laptop when it was delivered home with my gear.'

'I don't believe it!'

'Would I lie to you madam? Anyway, you wanted to know what happened at the swamp…'

Chapter 20

'We have to work with the army, we're being paid by the army, and Loot says he won't interfere.'

'That's as long as he approves our daily schedule,' replied Emma.

'May I suggest,' chimed in Oscar, 'that we give him the merest outline of our intended activities, then noting any reaction while we progress.'

Herb nodded in agreement with this suggestion and looked down again at the list that Oscar had asked him to compile regarding the standing stones that were in the mine at the first level.

'You noticed a pungent smell, like what?'

'Acrid, initially, and then sort of musty.'

'Like a short circuit across an electrical contact before it finally closes.'

'Exactly.'

'And the musty?'

'Sort of smell you get in some charity shops.'

'Or of care homes when you visit unexpectedly!'

Herb turned to Emma. 'This boy is good!'

A sharp retort was called for by Emma but Oscar quickly moved on; 'And flashes of light, like miniature starshells, shot out from the stones just before the big bang?'

Herb nodded.

'Then, after the bang on your way out, you're certain that the rock pieces you picked up came from the exploded standing stone?'

'Yes, I'm certain because Emma had been knocked down and was showered with them. I brushed some off and kept a few.'

They were in the stores tent, and had been since breakfast, with Oscar cross-examining them on what they could remember of the explosion on that first day.

'You must have enough facts for your report surely,' Emma complained. 'I feel absolutely drained!'

'I'll tabulate this over lunch,' was the reply, 'and see what conclusions fit.'

Earlier that day, together with a short list of planned activities, they had reported to Loot in the office. He, in turn, presented them with a current weather chart, a set of up to date radioactivity readings, and the expected air and road movements during the day. However Oscar had wanted to consolidate the events of the first series of disturbances at the mine with his own research and, for this, he needed the undivided attention of both Emma and Herb in close consultation.

So their planned activities were listed and approved.

They leaned against the tent poles as Oscar finished off and shut his laptop.

'This is just my own interpretation for our eyes only,' he said and handed them a stapled sheaf of a few papers. 'And the nuts and bolts of this is that I've collated what you've told me with some highly improbable, but definitely possible, geological events!'

After a quick perusal of his summary Emma and Herb were inclined to agree that he had made a very strong case for the mine to be immediately sealed with concrete and deemed *'place non gratia'* forever more.

Oscar had earlier sent the rock fragments for analysis and not only had they turned out to be quartz, containing minute pieces of quartzite from a rich gold bearing vein, but they had particles of human hair ebbed in a couple of them. He then contacted Charles Clark, who obligingly sent down a mouth swab, and the DNA of the hair and the swab were compared and a partial match obtained.

It had been assumed, quite correctly as it turned out, that there would have been a high degree of intermarriage in times past within the closed community at the mine. But even more startling was the fact that the body hair follicle appeared to have been alive within the last few months. The laboratory that tested the sample had no previous knowledge of where it had come from so Oscar rightly assumed that the results were correct and all above board.

These initial findings, together with Herb's observations coupled with the fact that quartz under pressure produces electric current (hence the electrical smell and shooting stars of light), led Oscar to surmise that the standings stones were not passive lumps of quartzite but restraints incarcerating that which lurked within. And the explosion that split the stone asunder could well have been one of these incarnates making its escape.

'I can see where you're coming from with this theory,' agreed Herb handing the papers back to Oscar, 'but this can't be possible in today's world surely!

'Do you mean to say that there's..?'

Emma paused in an attempt to rationalise her thoughts then tried again; 'Do you mean to say that there could be something wandering around loose down the mine?'

'The hair follicle was alive until quite recently and Herb is convinced that he saw something emerge from the stones after the explosion so until we can get back down the mine, and prove otherwise, that is my interpretation.'

There were no further comments and he concluded: 'It could well be dead or the idea so far fetched and beyond belief but that's how it stands at the moment.'

'So sealing the mine with tons of concrete, and keeping well away for the next thousand years or so, may not seem such a bad idea!'

'And it'll save us trying to explain this to an outside world,' said Oscar.

'A world unable to grasp the enormity of this unfolding drama and plunging headlong towards Armageddon,' added Emma jumping up somewhat theatrically after which she blushed and sat back down again looking slightly embarrassed.

'That was a dramatic statement my dear,' announced Herb unable to resist such an opportunity to respond, 'and it could well be the start of a brand new career move for you and yours!'

'And what might that be?' she asked aggressively while ignoring Oscar's raised eyebrow that obviously signalled the message that Herb was winding her up.

'Did you ever hear of the bizarre sexual habits of the Navarrese Basques?'

'Who?' replied Emma rather too loudly.

'Well these monks, whilst on the Santiago del Compostella annual fun run and pilgrimage, completion of which guarantees them a remission of half their time off purgatory in the next world, would fit chastity belts to their mules and...'

'And what on earth has that got to do with me?' she interrupted.

'Don't even ask,' suggested Oscar. 'It's on Google so check it out later.'

He looked from one to the other, admiring Herb's ability to set Emma off, but the banter slowly ceased as reality set in and they settled down once again engrossed in their own thoughts. The implications of what they knew were enormous and they felt collectively helpless to do anything as who, in their right mind, would take the explanations seriously.

After a while though, and with no other suggestions forthcoming, Oscar slid his laptop into the bag, hoisted it over his shoulder, and walked out of the door.

Explaining their ideas to the world ceased to be an option for the group when it started to rain late afternoon. It got heavier as the evening wore on so thankfully most of the personnel were still awake, attending to the numerous leaks and drips that were always part of the joy of living in tented accommodation, when a further magnetic shift occurred followed by a worse deluge that soon flooded the immediate area.

After the upheaval had finally settled down a survey revealed that the land level surrounding the mine had sunk to a depth of two metres. It was almost a repeat of the previous disaster all those years ago and, as the water level remained high, the personnel on site were lucky to survive with what they could grab before their temporary offices and equipment slid through the deluge and into the abyss before their very eyes.

Emma smiled at Paul who was stretched out comfortably on the sofa, with Saffie, on the other side of the room.

'It seems as if we've never been away!'

All the personnel had been evacuated from around the mine and the surrounds declared a Military Training (Live Ammo) Zone. The authorities needed time to sort out the implications so a 'retreat and regroup' policy was the easiest option and the Defence Department had returned Emma, and Paul who had arrived just after the event occured, to the motel at Charters Towers. Paul's mother had recovered from the viral infection enough for her sister to take over the care and, as the cost of keeping Saffie in the kennels had escalated, he had collected the dog and brought her up with him.

Herb had phoned earlier that morning and told them that he had accompanied an Army Recovery Unit to the mine the day before. They had been delegated the task of salvaging what they could of the submerged equipment but, after a few half-hearted attempts with cranes and grappling hooks, they gave up when the risk of losing their Prime Mover was pointed out to the Officer in Charge.

The edges of the sour water billabong, now renamed *Hotskins,* turned out to be of quicksand constituency and, if the Recovery Corporal from the Engineers hadn't demonstrated how the rocks he had thrown along the edges quickly subsided from sight, they might well have lost the Scammel Tractor if it had taken up its designated position.

Herb admitted that it was a difficult situation and the most obvious option was to drill and sink concrete and steel pylons into the bedrock to build a stable platform to start from. This initial cost would be astronomical and for what.

The Defence Department and Onesiphorus had some big problems to sort out and Emma, Paul, and Herb hoped they would be retained in their present position for some time to come as the next few weeks could be most interesting.

Chapter 21

'What the hell are they doing on Innisfail?'

'The local police discovered them arguing on the beachfront and took them into custody before transferring them to an illegal immigration centre.'

'Jesus! Let me think...'

After a few moments he pushed the intercom buzzer on his desk.

'Tell Gwen Fortesque I want to see her now!'

Keith Harding was the C.E.O. of Onesiphorus Mining and, until that phone call from one of the company's surveyors who happened to be in the Cairns area, he didn't think it possible that the situation at the mine could get any worse.

A call came in at the Police Station that a group of Asiatic originates, all in bright orange overalls and hardhats, were arguing loudly on the beachfront and a large crowd of interested early morning joggers and surfers were starting to gather.

The police duly arrived, took the eight men into custody as it was assumed they had been landed from a fishing boat or similar without the benefit of Customs and Immigration clearance, and took them to a temporary detention centre that, during normal hours, was the local Servicemen's Club!

Their overalls bore the company's name on the pocket, but embossed in a Japanese script, and it was fortunate that a Customs Officer on duty that day understood the language enough to obtain the relevant details. Although they worked for a Japanese company called Mandora Pi Exploration, who in turn were sub-contracted to manage the mine at Native Dog Creek, they were sponsored by an Australian company and Keith Harding was the person alerted when the police contacted the Brisbane office.

His day spiralled rapidly downwards from that point on but thankfully his able secretary, Monica, was on call and noted from the schedule that a mobile sampling drill rig, contracted to the company, was operating somewhere on the North Queensland Coast. She got through to the relevant department and, on discovering that one of their own surveyors was working with the rig team, she passed this information, and the name of the motel where he was staying, on to her boss.

It took a little while, over half an hour in fact, for someone in the motel reception to answer and, when they did and Monica could hear the phone ringing in the guest's room, she naturally enough switched the call over to her boss.

Luckily the surveyor hadn't left for work but unluckily he was in the shower and a local lady, who he'd picked up in the bar at the 'Dance of the Desperate' the night before and persuaded to stay over, picked up the phone and then, thinking it was room service, proceeded to give her order!

This was when Keith Harding reached the point of going absolutely ballistic and, if it was possible for the situation to get any worse, the lady concerned definitely didn't like the tone of the caller's voice, or the language he was using, and promptly hung up the phone.

Monica eventually wrenched control from her apoplectic boss and wasted another half an hour waiting for the motel reception to answer before finding that the gentleman concerned had left, somewhat hurriedly, for work.

She finally managed to contact him through his mobile. Her request to check out such an unusual occurrence, that was way outside of his usual duties and tasks, was only agreed upon in return for a promise that no further action would be taken on his misdemeanour and, more importantly, not a word would be breathed to his wife or family!

It took a certain measure of diplomacy but, as usual and as expected, Monica handled the task superbly.

'Where is she?'

'At Brisbane Airport to collect her brother Mr Harding. I've paged her and she's driving back into the City.'

'It's like some Crazy Gang Farce gone troppo...'

'What is Mr Harding..?'

Monica's question was cut short by Gwen Fortesque's sudden appearance at the office door.

'Be a dear Monica, two large coffees and some of those chocolate digestives!'

Gwen waited until the secretary was out of earshot before dumping an armful of folders on to the desk and sitting down.

'We have to get this bloody well sorted...'

'I know and there's no need to use your pithead

language with me. Wait until your secretary gets back and then send her out, we cannot afford to be overheard.'

She soon returned with the order, placed the tray on the desk, and then asked if there was anything else; 'No, take an early break Monica. Mrs Fortesque and I need to sort through a few problems so switch the phone back to the switchboard and I'll page if I need you.'

'I'll be in the laboratory then,' she replied and walked out shutting the outer office door firmly behind her.

Gwen Fortesque brushed an imaginary crumb from her skirt then smoothed an imaginary crease before dipping into her handbag and emerging with a tube of skin rejuvenator. She removed the cap, squeezed a portion onto her palm, and slowly replaced the cap before proceeding to rub the cream thoroughly into her hands.

'Now Keith, there's no need to take that tone with me.'

'I understood it was a straight deal, an old flooded mine that had possibilities!'

'I didn't want to bother you with the small print.'

'I thought we'd leased some army land for exploration and evaluation which sounds pretty straightforward to me'.

'That first set of problems occurred just when we had the place cleaned up and the water level under control.'

'That's a point,' he said and lit up a cigarette. 'How is Jim Saidler?'

'I wish you wouldn't smoke when the air-conditioning is on,' she replied jumping up to open a window. 'It makes my clothes smell awful...'

'I asked how Saidler was!'

'As well as can be expected,' Gwen replied sitting down again, 'although the doctors can't say when he'll be fit enough to return to work.'

'It's taken a hell of a long time for them to sort it out. You'd better let me have his latest medical report in case the Board asks any questions.'

Gwen scribbled Keith's request on a pad and looked up.

'Anything else?' she asked.

'Anything else! Anything bloody else!' He stood up so fast the chair fell over backwards and he kicked it viciously away behind him.

She looked on in amazement at this outburst; 'What on earth...'

'Don't you know! Don't you know what's happened at the Mine?'

'I know they've had more problems...'

'Problems aren't the word I'd use my dear Mrs Fortesque,' he answered, settling the chair upright and taking a deep breath before sitting down again.

He then leaned forward to emphasize his next statement; 'Bloody big disaster is more of an apt description that comes to mind!'

'Surely the Mandora Pi Team are sorting out these minor setbacks.'

Gwen's belief in her own infallibility was, from that point on, irrevocably dented by the reply; 'Not when the whole bloody lot of them has been washed up on the beach above Innisfail!'

Emma put down the phone and called out to Paul who was out on the verandah sifting through a pile of papers; 'Oscar's picking up Herbie before lunch, doing something at the library, and then they'll be calling in here after that. He wants to clarify a few things so I suppose he'll be hungry. Be a dear and put those sausages in the oven!'

The mention of the word sausage brought Saffie in from the garden just as one of the motel cleaners appeared at the unit door and handed Emma a letter; 'It was left for you at reception Ms O'Sullivan.'

Emma turned the envelope over in her hand. There was no stamp or address so it must have been delivered by hand.

'Did you see who left it?'

'No Miss,' replied the cleaner. 'It was just left on the counter.'

'Thanks,' replied Emma somewhat absent-mindedly and opened up the flap.

'I don't believe and yet I do!'

'If it's true then your teleportation theory is the only one that fits.'

Emma was answering Oscar's reaction to the contents of the letter. The writer, the same person who sent the audio tape, revealed that the eight members of the Mandora Pi team had been found alive and well on the beach above Innisfail and one of the company's surveyors, who happened to be working in the area, was handling the local details and had booked them into a beachfront motel.

The writer had no idea how their presence so far away from the mine could be explained away but as they were in the country legally, with the required visas and work permits anyway, it would just be a formality as they had broken no law. Gwen Fortesque had arranged a private charter and was flying up there personally to bring them all back down to Brisbane.

The letter went on to state that the writer continued to pray that the mine be returned to its original state and that her ancestors, once again, be left in peace.

They sat for a while as it took time to digest the news and the only activity was Saffie slowly circling the group hoping for a sausage hand me down.

'I've got an idea,' said Herb and walked out into the garden to use his mobile.

'How come there was nothing on the news or in the paper about it?' asked Emma standing up to clear the plates and carrying them to the kitchen.

'Maybe illegal immigrants have ceased to be newsworthy as no one's drifted in by boat for a while with their teeth filled with gold and their suitcases filled with Gucci Originals. The detention centre on Nauru seems to have solved the problem hopefully once and for all.'

'The plane won't leave Brisbane until early tomorrow,' announced Herb coming in from the garden. 'I'd love to go up to Innisfail and see how Mrs Fortesque handles the situation.'

'Maybe we should,' suggested Oscar. 'Because once they're in Brisbane they'll be hightailed out of the country as Gwen baby will make sure of that.'

'How long would it take us to get there?' asked Emma.

'Three or four hours,' answered Herb, 'and I know a few people in the yacht club there and Bob Jefferies, the Police Sergeant.'

'What are we waiting for then?' said Oscar with a huge grin. 'We can be up there today and rent a cabin in the camping ground.'

'What about the army. What if they try and contact us and we're not here?'

'Nothing will happen before Monday,' Oscar assured Emma. 'And if the water level at the mine remains constant next week then you will be declared *surplus to requirements* and returned to Brisbane.'

'So lets do it now!' was the unified reply.

Chapter 22

It was later that afternoon before they finally left. Paul elected to stay behind as his mother wasn't too good and he might need to fly down to Brisbane at short notice. So that left room in the Range Rover for bedding and essentials and also for Saffie who was always up for an adventure.

The journey to Innisfail was uneventful, not a lot of traffic, and they were soon sat in the Yacht Club with Bob Jefferies. Herb had phoned the Police Sergeant earlier and he'd picked them up at the camping ground after they had booked in.

'You were the last person I expected to hear from!' Bob remarked after he'd signed them all in and had settled down at a table. 'After you sold your boat I thought the Coast had seen the last of you.'

'When I first got it,' explained Herb to the rest, 'I had plans to sail her every free weekend but other things got in the way and it ended up being just a hole in the water into which I poured my hard earned dollars!'

'Aren't all boats like that?' answered Bob with a laugh. 'Anyway what brings you up this way?'

'Let's get another round of drinks and we'll tell you all about it.'

'The Army finally took them into custody and off they went.'

With that closure Bob sat back, looked around the

group, and then purposely drained his glass. Earlier on Emma had outlined her sequence of events starting with the abnormal audio sounds during the initial filming, and then Herb filled in any relevant bits finishing with Oscar's more technical overview of the current situation. They omitted to mention Gwen Fortesque's intended visit however and were conscious of the security issues so they were careful what else was said.

It took a while, and a couple more beers plus Herb's assurance that the information wouldn't go any further, before Bob revealed that which later turned out to be common knowledge around the town.

Evidently the interpreter in the area, a young woman named Donna who had studied for a hospitality diploma that included a six month stint in Japan before she joined the Customs, was quite adequate on the tourist side but somewhat lacking in the technical aspects of the language. Once she'd found out that they worked for a mining company, on a project a couple of hundred miles away and that they were in the country legally, her assurances that everything would be OK and they were free to go, reduced the level of conversation to where the spokesman of the group repeated the same answer to all her questions; 'Thank you for your interest and concern, the company will soon be here to collect us!'

The Police, Customs, and Immigration were in somewhat of a bind. The Japanese hadn't committed any offence, a major mining company was vouching for them and faxing up copies of their work permits and visas, and they weren't causing any problems so they were released. The surveyor, still tending to over-compensate for his misdemeanor in the eyes of the company, booked them into a beachfront motel and, on the instruction of his boss, left an open tab account on the company's credit card for their personal use.

The Japanese then proceeded to drink the lounge bar dry while the locals, who normally viewed all foreigners with suspicion, carried on as usual and the general opinion was that the group had stopped off at the beach for a swim and someone had pinched their car. However the following evening an army officer arrived in a jeep, together with an army minibus, and parked outside the Police Station. They activated the night bell and it was over an hour before the Inspector arrived. The Customs Officer, who handled immigration outside of normal office hours, was then summoned and together they went down to interview the Japanese.

The lounge bar was lively, the bush jug band noisy, and the locals warming to the foreigners who were well into their cups and buying drinks all round. One was dancing on the table while another, of small stature, was partially lost from view between the enormous breasts of an even more enormous woman. The army had brought its own interpreter but his attempts to interview failed miserably and a fight broke out between the soldiers and the bar security staff eventually spilling out onto the garden. Interested spectators, mainly respectable couples taking the air and enjoying their evening stroll but also a smattering of the town's yobs looking for trouble, then started to gather on the road outside.

The Inspector, a Vietnam Veteran of the Military Police, sensed that the situation could easily turn into a riot so he unsheathed his revolver and fired two warning shots in the air. Without further ado the crowds dissolved, the music ceased mid beat, the man of small stature released from his warm and snug cocoon, and the rest of the lounge fell silent. The soldiers accompanied the Japanese to their rooms, to retrieve their overalls, hard-hats and any other gear and then, after signing out at reception, they were escorted onto the minibus and locked in.

As the convoy moved off the Inspector walked over to the jeep and queried the reasons for the evening's activities; 'Just for the official report you understand?'

'The counter terrorism card,' answered the officer with a grin. 'It covers a multitude of sins!'

Chapter 23

After this wealth of information another round was definitely called for and Oscar soon returned with a tray of drinks together with a large bowlful of crisps.

'This army officer,' enquired Emma to the Sergeant, 'you didn't happen to get a name I suppose?'

'Larson, Lawson or something like that and I think he was listed as a half colonel on the Inspector's report so they must have thought it important.'

Emma saw a flicker of alarm in Herb's eyes and she steered the subject away from personalities; 'How did the Army know the people were here and why wasn't it mentioned in the media?'

'It was mentioned on the news but only in the context that a few boat people seemed to have drifted ashore. So I suppose the Immigration would have passed on the information to Army Intelligence so they acted on it.'

Bob dropped them off back at the camping ground and Saffie, who'd been left to guard their belongings, was dying for a piddle and wandered off into the bush directly the door was opened. They thanked the Sergeant and promised to make contact before leaving but, once inside the cabin, they brewed the coffee and sat around the table pondering their next move.

'It's a bit pointless hanging around here with the team in army custody.'

'I agree,' replied Oscar, 'but aren't you just that wee bit interested in what happens at the motel when the cupboard is found to be bare?'

'Surely she wouldn't just arrive, she'd contact the surveyor or phone first..?'

'I'd like to lay a bet, a fifty dollar evens stevens, that our so bloody efficient Mrs Fortesque will charter the aircraft, arrive at the motel in a taxi or two, and just assume that the Mandora Pi Team are patiently waiting to be collected.'

'We'll have some tucker here before we do anything, I'm famished.'

Oscar pulled up outside the *Tregrosse Café* and cut the engine. They had all slept reasonably well in the cabin and, early that morning, had driven north to where the Japanese had appeared on the beach. Herb phoned his mate at the airport on his mobile to find that the flight had left and was due to land after lunch.

The Café was back from the beach and a few people were sat outside, some reading newspapers but most seemed to be just sitting and being. Emma found a table and dusted the sand off of her seat before adjusting the sunshade.

'Coffee and hot rolls for all?' she asked the rest as a young woman approached the table. Herb nodded as Oscar scanned the menu and asked the waitress; 'What's this *'Cottage Pie with crust and rice'*?' She smiled shyly and explained that it was a special dish that her mother had created from minced lamb, nuts, raisins, and stuffed bananas.

'That sounds good to me,' was the reply. 'I'll have

a large helping, a couple of slices of toast, and a mug of tea.'

Saffie then put on her violent tail wagging spasm that guaranteed the attention of anybody in the food line. This occasion was no different and, after introductions were made, Rachel asked if Saffie would like some meat scraps from the kitchen. The dog reaction was positive so Emma put it into words; 'A few scraps would be greatly appreciated!'

Oscar laid his knife and fork onto the platter. 'That was spot on,' he exclaimed and sat back with a satisfied grunt. Herb had earlier got fed up watching Oscar feed his face so he wandered on down to the water's edge accompanied by Saffie.

'I wasn't on duty at the time,' she said stirring her coffee, 'but there were quite a few people about and they evidently sort of suddenly appeared.'

Rachel had finished clearing up the empty plates and wiping up the crumbs after which she joined them at the table with her coffee. Emma, who had initially enquired if the waitress had seen anything of the Japanese, then asked; 'Where exactly did they appear from?'

'From what I heard they came out from over there,' she answered indicating a stand of trees a short distance away that looked like an oasis. Oscar would remark later that it was like something you'd see on a middle eastern film set but was most unusual for around these parts.

'It's always looked a bit out of place but it seems healthy enough although the water tastes awful. There's a spring coming out from behind the rocks and various local weirdoes swear by its medicinal properties but the local council recently had it fenced off quoting some obscure Health and Safety Act.'

Emma and Oscar exchanged glances and both asked, almost at the same time, if it had a name.

'The local aborigines named it *Hotskins* and that's what it's called today!'

While Oscar moved his car along towards the spring and set up his water testing and other gear, Emma settled the bill and handed Rachel her business card before walking down to join Herb on the beach.

Saffie was having a fine old time with an Alsatian friend and they had acquired quite a collection of sticks, together with a few innocent bystanders willing to throw them into the water. As Emma approached Herb, who was paddling at the edge, she noticed how tired he looked and mentioned it.

'I'm still not recovered from that night on the piss with those lads from the Signals,' he replied with a grin and nodded towards the stand of trees where Oscar had parked the car.

'He's doing some tests on the spring water coming out the rocks,' she said, 'and I bet you won't guess what the aborigines call it?'

'How does *Hotskins* fit the bill?'

'You've got your phone switched on?' Herb asked as he climbed into the driver's seat. They had parked outside the motel, the one where the Japanese had stayed, and Emma and Oscar were about to enter on the pretence of meeting a friend but in reality to wait for the big eruption.

They had all agreed, earlier on, that it would be sacrilege not to have this auspicious occasion recorded from every aspect for the enjoyment of fair-minded players everywhere. Herb volunteered to cover the arrival at the airport and then follow the target at a safe distance but if there were any holdups he would text the details to Emma.

'You just worry about tracking Gwen,' she reiterated, 'and if anything out of the ordinary happens then you make certain you get it on either voice or video.'

'Yes madam,' Herb answered fastening the seat-belts on himself and Saffie, before starting the engine and slowly pulling away from the kerb.

'Grab that one by the door,' he said pointing along the side, 'and I'll get the drinks and some chips.'

Emma sat down to find that Oscar's choice of table had been the right one as they could observe the front entrance. The reception desk was in clear view and they were discretely shaded from public scrutiny by a few large pot plants. He soon returned with the order and immediately started on about the spring water.

'The samples I'll get analysed and the magnetic readings were nothing out of the ordinary except that, taking into account the magnetic abnormality of the place, they were on exactly the same longitude as the mine. This meant that if the team had been teleported then they had travelled along the south/north lines of magnetic earth force.'

'Have you met this Mrs Fortesque,' he asked suddenly, changing the subject and shaking some crisps into a bowl from a packet.

'Yes, at the interview.'

'What's she like?'

'Late 50s, medium height, well groomed and used to getting her own way!'

'Could that be her standing at the desk tapping her foot?'

Emma had been concentrating so much on the front entrance that she hadn't given the possibility of a *discrete rear access* any thought at all.

Oscar leaned over and switched on the voice recorder as Emma couldn't seem to decide which way to turn. He took out his sunglasses from his shirt pocket and handed them to her; 'Put these on, fire up the video then head towards the desk but don't get too close.'

Chapter 24

Gwen Fortesque, having suffered a restless night coupled with an early morning start, had indulged rather recklessly in corporate travel hospitality on the flight up.

She was swaying slightly while loudly berating the receptionist, who was pressing every button on her keypad desperately paging the duty manager on the intercom. But her message was being drowned out by a raucous voice repeating; *'They're...What!!!' 'They're...What!!!' 'They're...What!!!'*

The duty manager, a young lady of Mid-European extraction whose grasp on the English language was somewhat limited, eventually arrived to find the receptionist in tears and quite a crowd gathered in the reception area.

'What seems to be the problem?' she enquired, loudly accentuating every syllable of the question while quietly consoling the distressed receptionist with an almost mystical laying on of hands.

'You appear to have mislaid some of your guests.'

The manager flinched and stepped back, somewhat pointedly, at the strong aroma of gin on the breath of the lady making the statement.

'What guests might that be then Madam?' she enquired again.

'The Japanese group from Mandora Pi.'

'They booked out last night Madam,' she replied after walking behind the desk and scanning the previous day's diary page. 'Would you like me to check if we have forward booked any other accommodation for them?'

The lady took a deep breath. 'I suppose so but why have they gone?'

When the manager, who was scrolling through the reservations on the screen didn't answer immediately, the question was repeated but louder.

'Let me see if we have forward booked them first Madam,' she replied in her distinctive clipped English whilst attempting a reassuring smile, 'at one of our other most comfortable and economic motels!'

Thankfully at this point the Accounts Manager, whose account checking had been disturbed by the noise filtering into his office nearby, walked out and into the reception area. He had been in the hospitality trade for a number of years and had come across, and usually solved, many of the problems that arose in the day to day running of a motel.

'Everything alright Elki?' he asked looking around and identifying the source of the noise.

'Not really Mr Griffiths. This Madam has lost her Japanese guests and doesn't know where to find them.'

'God help us!' This cry of anguish, uttered from the lips of Mrs Fortesque who was on the verge of losing it, echoed around the area and out into the street.

'Would Madam like to sit down somewhere quiet?'

'No I bloody well wouldn't. I am the CEO of a huge mining conglomerate so stop calling me a bloody Madam!'

She shook off a condescending arm, a futile attempt by Mr Griffiths to steer her out of the public arena, and continued. 'I came up to collect your eight Japanese guests and, believe me, I will leave with them or know the reasons why!'

Accounts looked at Duty who gave a shrug of her shoulders.

'Will you please come into my office and let us sort it out.'

The lady stared at him before deciding that he was the more senior and bowed rather theatrically; 'Lead the way,' she said and followed him around the corner to accounts.

As Emma sat down, and returned the sunglasses to Oscar, Herb appeared through the door and asked; 'Anything happened?'

'Not really,' she replied, 'I videoed her at the desk but not much else.'

'Is she still here?'

'An older guy took her back to his office, said he'd sort it all out!'

'That should be...'

Herb's sentence ended abruptly as the older guy himself walked in and made his way to the bar. As he turned to survey the other customers, after giving the barman an order for two double gin and tonics to be taken to the lady in his office and a quick one for himself, he spotted Herb and went over.

'God almighty I thought you were dead.'

'Too much fight in the old boy yet Griff. How the hell are you?'

'Good, good. How's the good lady?'

'Still complaining... I'd like you to meet a couple of friends...'

With the introductions made they then chatted for a few moments until the barman walked past with the drinks on a tray.

'I've got to go...'

'What are you doing now?'

'I'm the Accounts Manager, mornings only usually but I seem to have encountered a problem.'

'It's not about your eight Japanese guests that's been mislaid?'

'How the hell did you know that?'

'We could hear that woman all over the motel shouting about her lost group!'

'I'd better take her this drink as I try to formulate an explanation regarding her missing staff.'

'Griff old mate! You seem to be the only person who doesn't know that...'

Herb interrupted his reply as Bob Jefferies, accompanied by a female police officer, looked through the door into the bar and saw the trio: 'I thought somehow I'd find you here. The receptionist activated the emergency services button on the switchboard and then, after realising who she had got through to, informed us that she was being harassed by a woman obviously affected by drink demanding the return of the Japanese tourists.'

'Do you know what happened to them?' asked Griff looking at the Police Sergeant. 'I'd be eternally grateful if you can get that woman off my back.'

'Last night's staff knew all about it, maybe they didn't think you important enough to pass on the facts!'

'Alright Bob Jefferies, you've made your bloody point, now what happened?'

'The army needed to talk to them so they took them away last night, in front of half the town, to somewhere quiet I assume!'

'And the lady in my office doesn't know?'

'Why should she? It's not the Army's job to reveal but the employer's job to keep track of their employees or contractors or whatever they are.'

With that news the Accounts Manager felt definitely more uncomfortable and looked at his informant somewhat balefully.

'Don't scan me with those come to bed eyes,' said Bob, 'and the answer is no!'

'What do you mean...?'

'You can tell her yourself, earn your film star wages for a change.'

He stood and picked up his cap then continued; 'And I'll carry on catching criminals!'

After another quick gin, Griff decided it was time to put the lady in his office out of her misery and those left at the table counted his steps to the office.

The number twelve was reached before he turned the corner and at number seventeen they heard the eruption as expected; 'They what! They're bloody where?' accompanied by loud threats of libel after which the security bells sounded causing mass evacuation of the building and the mustering of the local volunteer fire brigade together with other emergency services.

In her haste to depart Mrs Fortesque had broken through an alarmed fire door, jumped into the awaiting taxi, then out again just as fast after she'd quickly convinced herself that the motel was to blame and that the staff should locate, and return, the missing Japanese back to from whence they came!

Chapter 25

'No interruptions under any circumstances please Monica,' he instructed his secretary who quietly shut the door behind.

'Please sit down Gwen,' he said drawing in his chair and opening up the folder in front of him.

'I'd like to explain Keith…'

'Not Keith. It's Mr Harding…'

'But surely…'

'No buts unless it's your butt being propelled, at a great rate of knots, out of the company and out of my life.'

He immediately regretted his outburst, having promised Monica, less than an hour earlier, that he would hold his tongue and deal with this matter in a proper professional manner befitting his position, without resorting to pithead tactics but this woman…

'I've never been…'

'Spoken to like this?' The sentence was completed for her and he continued; 'Well you had better get used to it because you're finished.'

'Don't I get a chance…?'

'No, you don't. I was advised to give you, accompanied by security, an hour to clear your desk after which you were to be escorted out of the building but…'

'So I've got your kind and thoughtful streak to thank for not…'

'If you put it like that, yes but don't push it. You've messed up big time and the situation's getting worse by the minute.'

She uncrossed her legs and went to get up as if to walk out but Keith quickly ordered; 'Sit down; I need answers to some questions before you finally depart.'

Gwen Fortesque spotted this initial chink in her boss's armour as he wanted something from her so, if she used the subtle feminine weapons in her armoury, then she just might keep her job, or any job. She had given her all to the Company and couldn't afford to be dumped onto the job market at this time of her life.

'Look, I'm sorry,' she said very quietly and then told him a few facts about her meeting with Tom Epthorne and their subsequent arrangements. These revelations were accompanied by the hint of a sob and a slight shaking of the shoulder.

'I'm sorry too, I can see where you're coming from but that feminine ploy's not going to work with me. We have a very good chance that every mineral or other licences we hold, including the one for my bloody dog, will be cancelled by the Mines Authority.'

'Surely not…'

'Surely bloody yes for supplying information knowing it to be incorrect and misleading, when applying for an exploration and sampling licence.'

'Oh…'

'Added to that is a pile of court summonses for purposely withholding information regarding the Health and Safety layout of the mine that the Defence Department needed for access purposes during a Civil Emergency,' he paused then continued; 'Let me say it for you…Oh!'

'And,' he added, 'The fact that Defence doesn't own the land with the mines people conducting an enquiry to find out how they, and we, thought they did!'

He looked at her then away; 'This is a bad situation and, although I've always allowed you a certain amount of leeway regarding your position, you and this Tom Epthorne seem to have way overstepped the mark. You have never caused me any concern before but this seems to be a serious fraudulent scam and there's a bloody good chance we'll get the book thrown at us.'

'I had no idea it would turn out like this and I'd never knowingly risk damaging the company. I've been with you for over 30 years.'

'And,' she continued while dabbing her eyes, 'the shame and humiliation that I'm sure to suffer during that dreadful court appearance will haunt me for the rest of my natural.'

'It won't do the company much bloody good either and why did you introduce yourself as a CEO at the motel? A couple of the board members thought it was amusing that I was involved after reading the police report in the Courier. I had to put things straight in no uncertain manner!'

He looked down at the file and tried, albeit unsuccessfully, to hide the ghost of a smile as he remembered an accountant's comment that perhaps Mrs Fortesque should attend an anger management course sponsored by the company.

With these last few facts, and his expression, she sensed a softening of her boss's attitude so she took full advantage of the moment and said; 'I'll make a pact with you.'

He took off his glasses, rubbed his eyes, and sat back; 'I'm listening.'

'First of all I'll go, at any time you decide, taking complete responsibility for the whole debacle and keeping my mouth firmly shut.'

'Go on…'

'We are both good at our jobs but together we're bloody brilliant. Let me tell you the whole story and let's then plan a strategy so that the company's good reputation remains unsullied and neither of us are compromised by these past events.'

'I don't think we can get out of it that easily and what about all this paranormal and teleporting crap then?'

'Believe me that, as it doesn't fit into any known file at the Defence Department, then it will be shuffled around and ultimately mislaid.'

'Do you believe it?'

'I don't know what I believe but, at this point in time extracting the Company, and our good selves, from this situation is higher on my list of priorities!'

Chapter 26

They planned their strategy well over the next few days and, apart from a few minor misdemeanours and slaps on the wrist from the powers that be, managed to assure their shareholders that it was all a misunderstanding and that the majority of blame lay elsewhere.

The Japanese were released within a few days as they couldn't explain how they had ended up in Innisfail and the authorities had no idea how they got there. They had committed no crime so they were flown to Brisbane, collected by their agents, reunited with their belongings, and promptly returned to Japan.

The Mining Companies Legal Team looked into the charges of 'withholding information during a civil emergency when it was requested by the civil powers' and pleaded that the authorities had better access than the mining companies to documents and area maps as the leaseholder had only recently started to survey the site.

Onesiphorus' defence against the charge was that, when they commenced negotiations for leasing rights, they assumed that the area was either owned or managed in perpetuity by the Defence Department and, if this was not the case, then the lease should not have been granted in the first place.

The Defence Department, when the spotlight

swung towards them, admitted that an administrative error by the head of the section ensconced with the power to de-requisition, and the return of the land to its rightful owners at the cessation of hostilities in 1946, had failed to amend the records accordingly at the time and the present problem had stemmed from this point. The fact that the person concerned was long since retired and probably deceased, meant that no disciplinary action could be taken although enquiries by the Security Section were still ongoing.

However the public was assured that this situation would not occur again as the staff had been made aware of new guidelines being implemented. Within the Department itself the present personnel were encouraged to take advantage of the counselling facilities available after their shift if they had experienced any distress whatsoever by the negative media reports in the press. Mr Khan confided privately to one or two of his loyal staff that the fact that no-one actually asked for the land's return exonerated them and, whoever owned it, should be bloody grateful that Defence had continued to keep their eye on it for all these years and should be charged a land management fee!

The company admitted failing to put into place certain Health and Safety issues so, after a Junior Manager from that department was reprimanded and dismissed, this action satisfied both sides and the charges were withdrawn.

The cost of hiring the charter aircraft, plus associated travelling expenses including the three hour waiting time for two taxis during Mrs Fortesque's performance at the motel in Innisfail, was absorbed partially by constructive accounting but mainly by instigating a lawsuit against Mandora Pi. This lawsuit, citing criminal dereliction of duty by their employees deserting the workplace without putting certain safeguards in place, was finally withdrawn after an agreement, by the Japanese firm, to contribute to the legal costs and air-fares.

The national newspapers soon picked up the local media attention that Gwen Fortesque had attracted. Various explanations were offered which included a report from the Company Doctor that she had been suffering from a diet controlled diabetes for a number of years and, owing to the expected early departure of the flight, she had missed her breakfast and this had led to low blood sugar levels that resulted in a diabetic reaction at the motel.

If she had left the reception area when informed that the Army Security were interviewing the Japanese, quite voluntarily according to Defence, regarding their situation then everything would have been quickly forgiven and forgotten.

However her later verbal assaults on the staff, in the belief that they were to blame and should pay compensation for her wasted journey, followed by a physical one on Mr Griffiths when she took a swing at him and missed, had led to the police being summoned and the lady herself being taken into custody by the police and charged with drunkenness in a public place and wilful damage to motel property.

Her behaviour, aggravated no doubt by Mr Griffiths' constant replenishing of her drinks glass, had attracted a lot of attention and the local press, including Emma's video camera, had been on hand to record the event. She had, therefore, eventually been bundled into a police car, loudly threatening to extract retribution from all and sundry, before being driven down to the local lock-up!

Chapter 27

Tom Epthorne was the subject for discussion the following week when they all met up for a farewell lunch at Herb's house on the Sunday.

It was expected that this was the last time they'd all be together. Oscar had ongoing work with Defence as did Herb who was bringing the remaining Army equipment back from the truck park at the Mine and generally clearing up. Emma and Paul however only had a few more days of their contract left and would soon be returning to Brisbane.

The fact that the company and Gwen Fortesque had escaped any serious charges, although the latter was due to appear before the Magistrate later that month regarding the motel incident, further aroused the group and led to a spirited discussion on how best to nail Tom for his unethical behaviour.

Unfortunately the more they argued, with Herb acting as the Devil's Advocate, the more obvious it became on how difficult it would be to prove that he was guilty of any serious offence. Ideally it would be something that would link him directly to Onesiphorus but the way he had deftly used his own DMMC connections, plus Defence's obvious shortcomings in not de-requisitioning the land after the war, effectively shielded him from serious prosecutions and they all agreed it would be a waste of effort to pursue him for some petty offence.

Herb waited for a pause before bringing out a sheaf of papers from a folder.

'This is the background of the DMMC that I've finally put together with the help from all and sundry and other sources. I don't know that it's buttock clenchingly exciting as most of it we already know, but I'd like to go over it once again for a little light relief to aid our digestion after the delicious lunch ably created by my dear wife.'

Marie looked slightly embarrassed at one of her husband's rare plaudits but bowed to the accolades as she cleared up the remainder of the plates and carried them through into the kitchen.

Everybody welcomed the break in discussion so glasses were refilled and Herb, after adjusting the reading lamp, made himself comfortable in his favourite armchair and commenced by stating that, in his opinion, the whole episode had the makings of a bloody good story but, more importantly, other details might emerge or drop into place that the group were not previously aware of. He waited a few moments and then began his story.

Mathew Hopkins was appointed as Chief Witch Hunter by the Roundheads during the English Civil War and, as with any charismatic person in a position of power, he attracted quite a following of converts that gradually evolved into an extreme religious group. It was a period in history in the 17th Century when any person suspected of practising witchcraft, even on such flimsy evidence as having a friendly cat, was strapped into a ducking stool and dipped deep into the village pond with only a few surviving the ordeal.

However when the Royalists snatched the reins of power back once again from the Roundheads, the mood of the population changed and overnight the hunter became the hunted. By necessity the sect, as it had now become, quickly aligned themselves with the Pilgrim Fathers and escaped the supreme retribution by following them to the New World. Although chronicled as taking an active part in the Witchcraft Trials in Salem, there were no further records of them until they landed in Australia, at Moreton Bay, in the late 1860s along with the early influx of miners from the Californian Gold Rush that had effectively ended by then.

They survived initial persecution, failed in their farming efforts but succeeded in gold mining and, as with other extreme religions, their contact with the outside world was kept to the bare minimum and passing strangers never made it through the outer boundaries. The business flourished however and all went well until a direct descendant of the original witch hunter was elected Leader. This charismatic man, the result of an incestuous liaison of father and daughter, was gifted with the powers of persuasion while cursed with the stigma of his birth. He initially re-introduced the strict religious doctrine which had been relaxed somewhat over the years and the women folk, who had always worked beside their men in the mine, were relegated to menial tasks and household duties. This was achieved without too much resistance or protest so the Leader quickly reconvened the 'Witches, Elves & Devil Enquiry Panel'.

The first individuals targeted were the childless widows, deemed to be parasites and sinners for the very fact of being barren, who were dragged before the Panel and subjected to the ducking stool. This judgement was slightly different from the original concept however as this pond was filled with the acidic products from the gold extraction process. No one emerged unscathed and the victims were carried on the burial board, suffering the most horrifying burns and screaming in agony, to the acidic tailings swamp.

There the Leader cursed their souls before reading a few words from the good book in an act of forgiveness after which they were committed, most of them still alive, to the deep of the swamp where any remaining life was horribly extinguished and where their remains gradually dissolved over a period of time.

When the supply of widows ran out the mentally impaired females were then targeted followed by anyone who protested at the inquisitions. Thankfully these events ended abruptly one morning when a pocket of methane gas opened up during blasting operations, the secondary explosion ruptured an underground spring, and the mine was flooded. The settlement, built mainly around the entrance, quickly became submerged and a billabong came into being.

When the accident was eventually discovered it was too late to do anything and no one really cared.

It was eventually reported in the local press, which greatly emphasized the horrific details of the accident and the perceived gruesome sufferings of the victims, thus ensuring that the area was avoided by the general public at large.

That was until the water table in the area started to drop after the Atomic Tests in the 1950s and parts of the settlement became visible, although unrecognisable, as a thick layer of silt covered everything. Eventually the rains started to wash the mud away and the structural shapes, still visible today, rose to prominence after the deluge.

How the sect originally obtained the tract of land, SR3318, was through a convert called Daniel McGhee. Daniel was a corporal in the 63rd Regiment of Foot and took his *'Ticket to Leave'* at Townsville in 1864 and was given *'Soldier's Rights block number 3318'*. These blocks of land were supposed to encourage the retired soldiers to settle locally but the area was very harsh. This fact, together with very little ongoing support from the Government, led to most options not being taken up and the land reverted back to the Crown after 5 years.

The option on this particular block however was taken up but the project was short lived when Daniel's wife and eldest daughter died of cholera and he returned to Townsville where the rest of his children were put into care. Daniel, in his sorrow, took to drink and at one of the numerous temperance meetings in vogue at the time, he converted to the faith and joined the sect. In 1871 the D.M.M.C Company, with an address c/o The Rural and

Temperance Bank of Queensland in Townsville, registered a deed of mortgage pledging the title, SR3318, as collateral for the loan.

The mortgage was discharged in 1875 and there was no further mention of the company until 1887 when it was de-registered for failing to submit a yearly return to the relevant authorities.

The name, DMMC, was the initials of a sect called 'The Disciples of the Malleus Maleficarum Covenant'. In the 15th Century two Dominican Monks published a book giving advice on Inquisitional Techniques and worked examples of numerous collated horror stories both true and imagined. The reigning Pope at the time, Innocent VIII, gave them his blessing and the publication became the Witch Hunters Handbook and required reading for anyone wishing to excel in this profession. The hierarchy of the Catholic Church did nothing to rein in their excesses and it continued until well into the 18th century despite strong opposition from the numerous ecclesiastical authorities. One source described it as 'Open Hunting Season on Women' and estimated that nine million souls, mainly women, were horribly disposed of during this period between the 15th–18th Centuries.

Herb paused then looked up and asked; 'Any questions?'

'That certainly dots the eyes and crosses the tees!' said Paul before standing up to stretch and move his feet.

'In 1995,' continued Herb as he squared the papers and replaced them into the folder, 'the name

DMMC was resurrected as a charitable institution, then its status was changed to a proprietary company and then, in 1997, the business was re-listed as *'Material Handling Environmental Impact Studies'* and a PO box number in Townsville given as their address. Mark and Sophie Hopkins were named as board members along with one other with non-voting rights.'

'And that one other was *Mr Tom Epthorne!*' concluded Emma.

Chapter 28

'I don't know how the locals can cope with all that traffic day after day.'

Emma dropped her keys into the dish and slumped onto the settee where Saffie, albeit unsuccessfully, tried to scramble up beside her.

They had been back in Brisbane for a week and were working at the Enoggera Army Base on the outskirts of the City. The offer of continued employment with the Defence Department was quite unexpected but came about through a shortage of civilian staff in the photo-reconnaissance and mapping departments. During normal periods of increased work loads the army personnel, from an Engineers Topographical Squadron, would have helped out but they were all on large scale manoeuvres in New Guinea.

Both Emma and Paul were now temporary G/3 Clerks as, after phoning around the various agencies on their return to check out job opportunities in their own fields of which there were none, they had accepted Defence's offer on a week to week basic contract. Before they left Charters Towers Oscar had initially enquired if they had work on their return to Brisbane and then, when none materialized, he must have pulled a string or two.

However they were both grateful and the job, collating and filing information regarding coastal erosion and unusual occurrences on the north/east seaboard from satellite pictures, was both interesting and satisfying.

'So he wasn't the least amused to discover that he and Tom Epthorne were first cousins!'

Emma was telling Paul of the call she received from Charles Clark earlier in the evening, whilst he was out, regarding the results of his own enquiries into the earlier background to the Company and his own genealogical chart.

'They had the same grandparents but Tom was illegitimate with his mother dying in Sydney a few years later from a botched abortion,'

'Where on earth did this info come from?'

'Remember the research librarian you met in Bundaberg, George something?'

'Baxter or Baker.'

'Well he and Charles are friends, and he could even be one of 'The Circle'!'

'He didn't strike me as…'

'What do you think they should wear a special hat or badge?' goaded Emma.

'Look, don't get me started; just stick to the bloody subject in question.'

'Anyway,' she continued, tactfully retreating from a topic that usually escalated into a heated discussion, 'Tom was initially adopted out with a good family but traced Grandmother Emily in later years who helped support him through his university years for a degree in Accountancy. This was on the understanding that he would not contact any other member of the family as she still couldn't come to terms with the way her daughter had turned out—— and the guilt she felt in turning her out in the first place!'

'Well that goes some way in explaining Epthorne's motives and he may well have a claim on the Mine and surrounding land.'

'He might well have if the male and female lineage has equal status.'

'What do you mean?'

'Well Tom came from female/female and Charles from female/male which gives him precedence.'

'Oh,' said Paul then tried another tack. 'What about any other survivors?'

'A complete blank on Jed Wilberforce and the other possible.'

With that Emma went out to the kitchen to make coffee and to put a few biscuits out in the bowl for Saffie's supper.

'There was one other thing…,' she said returning with the two mugs and continuing; 'And don't forget that Luke and Maisie had another son, David…'

'That's interesting so other facts may still emerge'

'And the lady who sent me the tape and the note could well be from his lineage.'

'Food for thought,' replied Paul then shushed Saffie who had suddenly jumped up on hearing that word!

A few days later they had an unexpected visitor. Charles was in the area and had phoned early in the morning so, as they were both on the afternoon shift, he was invited around to Emma's place for coffee as soon as he could make it.

'I couldn't put it off any longer as I've started to loose sleep, these dreadful bags are filling out under my eyes, and that's really not my scene!' he announced on arrival and followed Emma through into the lounge.

Paul had some difficulty in keeping a straight face. He hadn't met Charles before but Saffie saved the day by barking at a convenient passing noise and Paul managed to compose himself.

Charles Clark switched to a serious mood.

'I met Cousin Tom for lunch yesterday and I'm seeing him again today to try to extract ourselves from this mess.'

'But this was none of your fault,' protested Emma.

'I know but my great aunt and uncle are involved, albeit innocently, and it would kill them if the case, which seems to have all sorts of complications, was dragged through the courts and they were summoned to give evidence.'

'Do you have time for another cup?' asked Emma.

Charles looked at his watch and stood up. 'Let me use your loo and then I'll give you a quick overview of my first meeting with Tom.'

On his return Charles acknowledged that the subject in question had not acted honourably but an overview of his earlier background might help bring his actions into some sort of context.

'When Tom eventually traced his grandmother or, should I say our mutual grandmother, he naturally expected to become part of the family,' Charles continued and settled himself on the settee. 'This was not to be however but I've got to digress a little to bring this into some sort of context so please be patient.'

He went on to reveal that the grandmother, a formidable matriarch with unshakable opinions of the time regarding unmarried mothers, had done her utmost to keep her daughter's pregnancy secret from the neighbours and the rest of the family. After the boy was born, and safely adopted out, she barred her daughter from the house forthwith and had no further contact with her.

The Clark family thus regained, once again, their cloak of respectability and the disturbing events gradually faded into the background until a parcel of clothing and a few oddments arrived at the house. Enclosed, with a covering note, was a death certificate and a demand for twelve pound, seven shillings, and sixpence, from the N.S.W Police for services rendered to the deceased.

The daughter had, in Sydney, died during a botched abortion and the couple who had performed the operation were apprehended as they were disposing of the body from the boot of a car into the harbour from one of the wharves. The couple then led the police to a shabby room in a boarding house at The Rocks where a search revealed a few papers which identified her together with the address of the family home. Several previous letters from the Police, after the event, had been ignored by the grandmother and these were enquiries asking if she was mother of Margaret Rose Clark and, if she was, would she kindly contact Sergeant Ian Booth at the Central Police Station in Sydney. No mention was made in the letters that her daughter was dead and, although she had her nagging doubts for a while, the correspondence was put to one side as the grandmother just didn't want to be involved and, anyway, her daughter's Christian names were Mildred Emily!

The Police must have got tired of waiting, and buried Mildred, or Margaret Rose as she was known around the local ale houses, in a pauper's grave, parcelled up her few belongings and forwarded them, together with the bill, up to the only address they had. When she opened the parcel, and a few faded family photos emerged, it was obvious that the deceased was her daughter and the subsequent guilt she felt nearly sent her over the edge.

Time heals of course but then, when young Tom turned up, the guilt started all over again. Her obsession with appearances, not the visual sort but the family's standing within the community regarding a certain level of respect and good character, was still firmly at the forefront. However she had mellowed slightly over the years and decided that she couldn't just turn her grandson away. She had never suffered fools gladly, or the weak willed, and remained convinced that any hurt caused through her actions was merely incidental and of no real consequences.

She still insisted however that Tom should have no contact with other members of the family but did eventually become quite fond of him and very proud when he passed his final exams even going so far as buying him a gold watch.

'I'll make some more coffee,' said Emma and went through to the kitchen.

'Your grandmother seemed to have played her cards pretty close to the chest,' commented Paul, 'and sounds like some sort of control freak.'

'I can't remember her saying a good word about anyone, and she scared me from a very early age, but thankfully my father was very understanding and made certain that we kept our mutual distances from each other.'

'How did Tom actually find out about the mine if he was alienated from the rest of the family for so long?' Emma asked putting the coffee tray on the table.

'It was during one of his earlier clandestine visits to the family home,' said Charles and continued with the story.

A scrapbook of cuttings detailing the mining disaster, and the family lines and connections, lay in the sitting room book case and Tom happened upon it at that particular time. At the earliest opportunity he stole it and it wasn't until after the grandmother died, aged 91 in 1992, that her son George shared his great concern, with his son Charles, at not being able to find the scrapbook which he considered an important family heirloom that should have been passed on to him.

His Uncle George's concerns were unknown to Tom however and, although he knew his uncle by sight, he respected his grandmother's wishes and had no contact with him or the rest of the family and it was only after reading the death notice in the paper that he learnt of her demise. As the funeral cortege left the house he stood unobtrusively outside on the pavement and later attended the burial, albeit standing well away from the family group, and paid his respects in his own quiet way.

By this time Tom was a senior partner in a large accountancy firm and the disaster story was all but forgotten. That was until he visited Charters Towers on business and took time off to explore the mine site where he immediately saw the potential of a mine that was in full production until the disaster had occurred. The first step was to register the name as he definitely had a claim, legitimate or otherwise, but he wisely kept the procedure out of the public domain just in case there were any other distant family members waiting to jump on the bandwagon.

When the price of gold reached record heights however Tom decided to take the next step in his overall plan of action and traced any other descendants of the original DMMC. They were his Great Auntie Sophie and Great Uncle Mark, who were well into their 90s, but he decided not to reveal the family connection when he visited them in Bundaberg where they were living in a nursing home. He knew, from past experiences, the value of a friendly female face when dealing with the elderly so he was accompanied by one of the secretaries. The meeting almost had the air of a family gathering as the couple were childless so, when Tom suggested the formation of a memorial society remembering the mine disaster and linked to his own research project, they readily agreed to become the society's patrons.

No mention was made by the couple however, of their great nephew who was living in the States at that time, and who didn't take up his power of attorney role until after the visit and on his return to Bundaberg. Although Tom was aware of a cousin's existence somewhere in the distant past, he failed to make the connection while Charles was ignorant of the whole situation.

The appropriate forms were signed by the couple after which the visitors took their leave, citing a busy schedule, but promised to visit again in the very near future. For the secretary the trip was just a pleasant day away from the office and, after being wined and dined at an expensive lunch followed by a late afternoon session in a highway motel, she conveniently forgot all details of the morning visit.

Almost all the signed papers were eventually doctored as required and the one that registered the elderly couple, as shareholders to the new DMMC Pty Ltd, was retained in Tom's private file. This gave the company, which now had on its books the defunct mine and surrounding acreage, a certain cloak of respectability. From that point on it submitted its yearly accounts to the relevant authorities including a series of test results from the tailing mounds dotted around the mine entrance, depreciation on basic tools, instruments, and even a tin shed on site. In fact all the essentials expected from a small outfit just ticking over in first gear waiting for the right combination of circumstances to arrive.

And then the main component suddenly surfaced, quite unexpectedly, in the shape of Gwen Fortesque and Onesiphorus Mining.

'You never knew of an Auntie Mildred or Margaret then?' asked Paul.

'I've been trying to puzzle out why,' he answered, 'and the only reason I can come up with is that my father must have lost track of his sister once she'd left home and that grandmother wouldn't allow the name to be spoken in the house. I can't recollect any mention of it although lots of conversations in that house seemed to end somewhat abruptly directly I entered the room!'

Charles suddenly stood up and smoothed down his trousers. 'Although I've always put that down to me suddenly appearing dressed up in my sister's clothes and screeching; 'Aren't I prettier than Dorothy?"

He smiled and waited until the laughter subsided before announcing; 'I've got to go but I hope I've clarified why I'm doing this as he had a pretty rough deal from the whole family and I'm certain that my parents must have known something and did nothing about it.'

'We can see your point,' assured Paul, 'but please keep us in the frame.'

'Of course but my first priority has to be to the family and that includes Tom, but I'll update you with an interim report and maybe phone this evening if we make any reasonable progress.'

With that they thanked him for the visit and walked with him to his car.

More than a week went by however before they next heard from Charles and his e-mail indicated that a satisfactory agreement had been reached with the DMMC Pty Ltd being switched back to a charitable status supporting an option for historical and religious research in the area. Charles also mentioned that another possible relative had been traced and he'd contact them again if anything developed.

'They've all come up smelling of roses so there's nothing left to be done.'

Herb's words on the phone said it all after Emma told him of Charles' visit, and the outcome. He sensed her frustration at the finality of it all so he tried his best to cheer her up with his latest news; 'Gwen's court appearance was a complete farce and she must have been incandescent at the magistrate's order to attend an anger management course and then to complete the community service hours.'

He heard Emma laugh so he added; 'It was all very well publicised so that must be some consolation to you.'

'Not the same as a three to five year prison sentence for fraud and plagiarising my research but I suppose it will have to do!'

She had been disappointed but felt at the time the need for a closure, to move on, so when Herb invited her and Paul up to Charters Towers for a few days holiday the offer was gratefully accepted. They would pass through Bundaberg on their way so they later contacted Charles, who sounded pleased to hear from them and who alluded to further snippets of information that they might find interesting. So they arranged to meet him later that week for lunch.

There was no problem taking a break from work as it was a slack period and the powers that be were only too glad to let them have time off, unpaid of course, although the mapping department would be busy again in a couple of weeks.

Their supervisor, when he heard they were calling into Bundaberg on their way up north and as a sweetener to ensure that his two good workers would return to the fold, arranged for them to transport some delicate measuring instruments to the local weather recording station. The shipment would not be ready for collection until the early afternoon which enabled one of them to claim two more days pay, an overnight stay in a motel, and a car mileage allowance both ways.

'I've booked at the Nanking again, it will be quiet and the food is very good,'

Charles had knocked on the door of their unit and announced that he had left his car at home as he was really looking forward to a good night out.

The journey up, that took a little over 3 hours, had been uneventful and they delivered the instruments to the weather station at Bundaberg Airport where the delivery note was duly signed confirming that the items had arrived in an undamaged condition with the seals intact.

'Rather swish place you've here,' remarked Charles looking around the lounge.

'The Defence Department does not skimp on the comfort and well being of their staff and they gave us a double unit for the price of a single once we explained there were two of us!'

'It all sounds a bit complicated but you seem to have landed on your feet?'

'Not really as we're only temps but it's interesting and will do until media jobs in our own field start surfacing again.'

'Right,' said Paul jumping up from his chair. 'Let's go eat!'

Chapter 29

'And when Baxey Boy came up with that research gem that Tom and I were cousins you could have knocked me down with a feather!'

They were waiting on their main course having deliciously dawdled over the other two, together with numerous bottles of wine, and were thoroughly enjoying themselves. Charles was at his campingly best, funny but not embarrassingly so and although he consumed more wine than the other two put together, he still kept his faculties and was spot on with most of his statements and replies. He was obviously well thought of by the restaurant staff, and many of the customers, and both Paul and Emma felt comfortable in his company.

A lot of exhaustive research from sources in Australia and beyond had been carried out, he revealed, but the results had confirmed that there was no trace of any other possible survivors from the disaster and no further trace of Jed Wilberforce since the mention of him, in the news-sheet dated 1895, standing in at Luke and Maisie's wedding to give the bride away. The couple were mentioned in the 1901 Census and, although Grandmother Emily was born that year she wasn't listed so she must have been born after the data collection. Jed wasn't mentioned either in that area although George Baxter might turn up something at a later date.

'So we can safely assume that the only issues living today are Tom, and myself of course, plus two probables and their offspring.'

'You never cease to amaze me,' said Emma. 'Were the probables from your Uncle David once removed?'

'No,' he replied shaking his head. 'He succumbed to TB, or was it flu, in the early 20s and left no issue.'

'Well?' They both asked in unison and leaned forward expectantly.

'I won't get confirmation of their identity for a day or so and I'll let you know soonest but maybe you can help me on something in return?'

With that Charles emptied the bottle into Emma's glass, signalled for another, then sat back and asked; 'I'm wondering if you know anything about the helicopter which disappeared in the Native Dog Area? It belonged to Channel 3-1Y and a neighbour of a friend of mine was on board.'

Emma and Paul exchanged glances as they had previously listened to Herb's disc and both found it difficult to believe the sequence of events. By his account the machine had lost power, no doubt through the influence of the magnetic field, and had come down on the edge of the swamp. The pilot and TV crew appeared shaken but relatively unhurt and, although the rotor gearbox had been ripped off, the main body of the machine remained comparatively upright. One of the occupants partially opened the door, the effort of which rocked the unit, and that was when a movement on the surface was observed by the onlookers.

That slight disturbance suddenly erupted into a swirling vortex and an eerie mist arose as the swamp spilled over the edges. A number of near human shapes, seemingly covered with a ragged black blanket, gradually evolved from the mist as they advanced swiftly towards the fuselage, and the broken unit, before the door was quickly shut. The terror of the crew could be clearly seen as the shapes surrounded their prey and then only heard as the objective was finally cocooned.

At that point a couple of soldiers at the fence-line fainted while the corporal, who was earlier videoing his section at work, seemed to be rooted to the spot although most of the recorded detail of the incident was blocked out by the broken machinery and it was only Signalman Michael McGinnis who clearly observed the whole episode. A period of silence was followed by a loud slurping sound, as though the shapes were pausing for breath or amalgamating their efforts, before a clicking noise commenced almost like the beat of a drum. A larger spill came up from the swamp, as if to assist, and the complete unit was pushed and slid, together with the stricken crew, down to the very edge of the swamp and then in.

It lasted only a few minutes after which the shapes reverted to the spill, the spill drained back into the lake, and the surface settled down again to an eerie calm.

The Signal Unit, together with the video, were all flown out the next day. The Army closed ranks on this, as expected, so Herb's version was the only important record of what actually happened in the public domain. When they had discussed this, and the fact that Herb's laptop version of the event had been wiped, the Army experts who had accessed the hard-drive must have noted that three CDs had been cut from the file. And it would have not taken a great degree of intelligence for the powers that be to work out who the discs had been for, so these facts resulted in them being squirreled away to a place where only Saffie was a silent witness!

Almost in unison Emma and Paul shook their heads and denied any knowledge of the query. They had, after all, ongoing employment with Defence and were still subject to the official secrets act, but their secondary consideration was that they had no idea what Charles might do with the information and who might get caught up in any aftermath.

'When you are in a position to tell me then I would very much like to know,' he remarked sounding somewhat disappointed but left it at that.

The glace fruits arrived at the table and, with their wine glasses replenished, Charles continued with the story of his earlier meeting.

Tom Epthorne had been almost suicidal as the Saga of the Mine unfolded and firmly convinced that he would be made the scapegoat of the whole sordid affair. However when the cousins first met, and a possible solution suggested that might sort out the mess, the floodgate of emotions had opened up and the whole sorry sequence of events disclosed.

'It was so embarrassing,' said Charles selecting the last of the cherry fruits that Emma had had her eye on. 'There we were seated at a corner table, thankfully somewhat discrete in an alcove of one of the better Italian restaurants, when the poor man burst into tears!'

'I still can't feel sorry for him at all,' said Paul, 'although I think suicide would be a bit drastic.'

'Anyway,' was the reply, 'let me carry on or else we'll be here all night!'

Charles went on to tabulate a series of points that followed that first meeting between Gwen and Tom and what he revealed went a long way in filling the gaps of what they already knew.

When Emma's initial application regarding the mine was received at the Heritage Offices in Brisbane, Geoff Donaldson took it home to study and found it fully suited the criteria. He passed it to Gwen Fortesque on the Wednesday for her approval and, whilst giving it a cursory perusal during her coffee break, she immediately saw the potential and proceeded to act. Information was gathered from various sources which culminated in a visit to the Registrar of Companies, after lunch, and then on to the Mines Office to double check certain relevant details for herself.

Emma's research was very impressive and Gwen, on her return, spent the rest of the afternoon reading through it and crosschecking the facts. On finishing she quickly took the initiative and, in her position of DCEO of Onesiphorus Mining, called an emergency meeting of the board that very evening. She had done her homework well and presented a case that risked a miniscule amount of capital for the opportunity of good returns on their investment. The mine had been in full production until the flood so, with modern pumping and draining methods, it could well be in full production again. The board realised that here was a rare opportunity to re-work a mine that very few people knew about, and that hadn't been 'dug out', so they voted unanimously for Gwen to handle the ground work.

The next day her P/A contacted the registered offices of DMMC to disclose Onesiphorus' renewed interest in the area, thus inferring that they had been involved in recent explorations there which was wrong, whilst mentioning that an abandoned mine had been noted which was believed to be in the DMMC portfolio.

The P/A reported back that Tom Epthorne wasn't the slightest bit interested in any proposal whatsoever, in fact he was quite abrupt, but to Gwen this was a minimal setback and Tom soon found himself sharing a table for lunch, at one of the more exclusive restaurants, with a lady who refused to take no for an answer!

Tom however was very wary and although he was convinced that his initial actions regarding the mine weren't really criminal, after all he was a direct descendent of one of the survivors and the facts were clearly listed in his grandmother's scrapbook, he was concerned that his subsequent business ethics appertaining to DMMC, and the manipulation of the elderly couple to become board members, would not stand up in a Court of Law so he had to be extremely careful.

'So Epthorne knew that he was on dodgy ground?' Paul asked, 'and his motives weren't solely based on the fact that he was the lawful descendant and the rightful owner of the mine.'

'He knew exactly what he was doing, and it very nearly came off, but let me tell you about when Tom first met Gwen!'

Gwen shook out her napkin, laid it across her lap, and looked up at the man sitting opposite: 'I didn't really know what to expect but it's obvious that you will not succumb to flattery so I shan't bother!'

The summing up, within their first few minutes of meeting, had been spot on and from that point the meal progressed satisfactorily with each recognising in the other a willingness to lay any scruples to one side for the sake of material gain. By the time coffee was served they had discussed a plan that could come into fruition if certain criteria were met. Gwen had wanted an answer immediately but Tom insisted on more time to ponder, and to put one or two safeguards into place, so he agreed to contact her by noon the next day at the very latest.

After leaving the restaurant he called in at the Mines Office and asked for the Folio in question. He had accessed it before but further examination on certain aspects was one of the tasks on his list and he noticed that the area SR3318, the block that included the mine, had been requisitioned in 1939 and incorporated into the much larger adjoining area LX1130 that was already owned by Defence. He studied it for a while and gently tapped his pencil, a habit that usually preceded a decision, before shutting the folio and returning it to the desk.

Settled into his office he immediately phoned Defence asking for the land leasing section and was connected to a most helpful lady. He enquired about the procedure for leasing Defence land and, after a few leading questions, the lady revealed that a film company had had a short term lease recently on the larger block which included the mine.

This was news to Tom but a statement by the father of Sir Thomas More came to mind; 'Never interrupt your enemies when they're making a mistake!'

He needed time to think so he thanked his informant profusely and rang off.

'No calls for ten minutes,' he told his secretary and then, behind closed doors and seated at his desk, he picked up a pencil and started to list the facts.

The Defence Department, according to the records, had evidently never de-requisitioned the smaller block after the war and so, when no-one had enquired about it since the war, it had been gradually incorporated it into the larger block LX1130. Apart from a few tour parties which he was aware of, and some army manoeuvres that had ceased some time back, nothing much had happened in the area until the film company made that first enquiry.

It was a genuine mistake on Defence's part to grant a lease for land they didn't own, and the person handling the application should have double checked the land records, but nevertheless Tom realised that it was a fact that could definitely be used to his advantage by keeping himself, and DMMC, out of the limelight for as long as was needed.

Aligning the pencil on the desk beside the blotter, adjoining a few of its kind, he took the business card from his pocket and paused for just a moment before leaning forward and dialling the number.

Paul's visit a day or so later was unexpected but Tom took it as an omen and called into the Mines Office once again. This time he took with him a small bottle of whitener and finally erased all record of SR3318 from the chart. From that moment on, to the untrained public eye, the smaller block ceased to exist and the Defence land increased by a hundred or so acres. In addition the original charts were soon to be scanned for microfilm thus making the erasure permanent as far as any future viewing was concerned.

'And we have it on a two by five year lease with right of renewal on LX1130, all for a peppercorn rent.' Gwen sounded delighted. 'We'll honour the financial arrangement, as discussed, and it's your turn to take me out to dinner.'

He laughed and replied. 'When my first consultant's fee arrives I'll be glad to.'

'Thanks again Tom,' she said and rang off.

Chapter 30

They were all comfortably seated in the lounge and Charles gave a loud sigh of satisfaction as he slumped back into the chair. Emma's suggestion, as they left the restaurant earlier, that they all went back to the motel for coffee was well received.

'I don't think I've met anyone with the capacity to tell a story, to hold everyone's attention, and to hit the relevant fact right on the button every time.'

He acknowledged Emma's plaudit with a slight nod of the head and continued to sip his coffee; 'I have several columns in the dailies and more weekend paper work than I can handle but I do enjoy a good food blow out and the company of people who appreciate my stories such as your good selves!'

'We knew some of it but my attitude towards Tom Epthorne has possibly mellowed slightly,' said Emma, 'although I've never actually met him.'

'I found him arrogant,' interrupted Paul, 'and a bit too sure of himself.'

'Admit it,' goaded Charles. 'You didn't enjoy being taken for a fool.'

'I didn't but he got his comeuppance and that's some compensation.'

'He's not a bad bloke considering the rejection he'd suffered and he's still a switched on guy who, I'm sure, will survive. So this charity research reinstatement for the DMMC could be a winner. The Oldies aren't fully with it so I've used my power of attorney to proceed as I see fit. An option was to fold the company which I, or we, didn't think a good idea as it has got a lot of earning potential.'

'For mining?' asked Emma.

'Of course not but, with its history and a little help from the media, it could become a premier tourist destination.'

'How will you handle the army's presence then?'

'We are sorting that out now and Defence will eventually back off.'

'Wouldn't it make a fantastic adventure film?' enthused Emma.

'Funny you should say that...'

Charles had dropped off to sleep in the lounge so they left him to it and went off to bed. When they awoke next morning he was gone so they departed right after breakfast and drove further up the coast as far as Sarina where it took time to find a motel that took dogs. An early start the next day had them heading for Townsville and then on to Charters Towers where they arrived late in the evening and very tired.

'And that's all he told us.'

They were settled back into the motel and describing their evening out in Bundaberg. Although Herb had invited them for a few days his wife's health wasn't too good, a hornet sting on the foot having led to a shock reaction, so he had negotiated an inexpensive few days break for the couple.

'Since they've changed DMMC's status back to a charitable institution that intends using the tourist dollar to fund research and renovation of the old mining sites, then the tourist slant is a good idea especially as Charles is well known in both the media business and the gay community.'

Herb leaned forward and opened another beer. 'And as a bonus he has an accountant as a partner so how can they lose?'

'Do you think the idea is good because you may be involved in the near future?' asked Emma sensing an opportunity to enlighten the conversation.

'I'm a good driver and know the area so I'd be the natural choice,' he replied somewhat mischievously. 'Although, on second thoughts, Lefty Carson might be a better choice as I've always reckoned he's a bit that way inclined!'

'Now that statement could be viewed as xenophobic…' Her ringing mobile interrupted Emma's retort and she walked through to the bedroom. While she was away the pair discussed the present situation on what had come to light and how neatly the guilty pair had side stepped any responsibilities. They had taken a gamble and, although it hadn't paid off as expected, they had got away without suffering any of the serious consequences.

'Do you remember a Janet Metcalfe, Basil Johnson's secretary?'

Emma had walked back through into the lounge and asked Herb the question.

'Not really, only the couple of times I've been to see Basil. Why?'

'That was Charles on the phone. He's just had confirmation on the state of play of a couple of estate contenders.'

'What estate?'

'Did you know any Janets at school?' she asked Herb ignoring Paul's query.

'There was one, a class or so below me, but I knew her brother better as he was in my year before the family moved away.'

'Any idea where they went?'

'Back home to Townsville I think. Their father might have been a geologist with one of the mining companies and was working out of Charters. What's this about anyway?'

Emma was obviously enjoying the subterfuge; 'Can you remember the surname?'

'We used to call John Macgooey but his real name was McGhee...'

Herb paused as the inference became obvious.

'Surely not...'

'Yes sir! No other than Daniel McGhee's Great to the third Grandchildren!'

It was a while before anyone spoke and when they did it was everybody together. Oscar arrived in the middle of all this and Saffie joined in with a few well chosen barks, thus restoring the assembly to some sort of order so that a calm and civilised discussion could take place.

'How are the new partners handling it with this new input?' asked Oscar after Emma had brought him up to date with the latest revelations.

'As far as I can see,' she answered, 'Janet and John are in pole position regarding direct descendants, assuming the name McGhee goes back unbroken to the original recipient.'

'But weren't the deeds transferred to DMMC way back and used to secure a mortgage?'

'Maybe Daniel McGhee kept them in his name as they were only used for collateral after all.'

'Do they still have a valid claim after all this time?' asked Paul.

'Of course they could,' replied Herb, 'because as Daniel actually worked the block for a while it remains in the family in perpetuity.'

'So,' concluded Emma, 'as long as the blood line fits the criteria then John and Janet are the front runners!'

Oscar, in the area for a few days to take the final measurements and water samples after which Defence wanted to scale down the project, then brought the group up to date with the present situation at the mine. Emma and Paul had thanked him for his input in finding them employment although he denied any involvement whatsoever but they knew different.

'What's emerged so far,' he commenced as he rustled through his briefcase and pulled out a folder, 'is the fact that there has recently been a vast increase in the level of sunspot activity.'

'What does this mean in laymen's terms then?' asked Paul.

'Well the earth's magnetic field forms a powerful magnetic shield layered high up in the atmosphere to protect us earthlings from the intense cosmic radiation. Occasionally an extreme burst of energy, from the sun's generator going slightly off kilter, breaks through the solar surface and shoots a barrage of charged particles off into space. This is called a solar wind.'

He paused to ask: 'Everybody OK so far?'

'Just as an aside,' said Herb, 'I was reading about an early Greek microlite belonging to Daedalus that flew too near to the sun. It came unglued and father, together with his son Icarus who had hitched a lift, found themselves plummeting towards earth at a great rate of knots and all done without parachutes. Was the melting of the wax holding the joints caused by sunspots?'

'Are you having me on?' Oscar asked.

'Well did they?'

'Did they what?'

'Bloody well come unglued that's what!'

'Not that I know of,' he replied refusing to rise to the bait. 'Is it OK if I carry on then?'

'Yes of course.' Herb permitted himself a tight smile before leaning forward and interrupting Oscar yet again! 'I was talking to one of the gardeners who works in the Botanical Gardens; he keeps bees and has had trouble recently with his hives.'

'What sort of trouble?'

'The problems started when they wouldn't come out and, when they did, they couldn't seem to pick up a direction and some of them even flew into a wall!'

'I didn't know the effects had spread so far,' said Oscar, 'but the bees depend on the earth's magnetism for all their functions so this could equate with the 'Chaos Theory'.'

'Could you enlighten me?' enquired Emma.

'The loss of a beat of a butterfly wing changed the course of history.'

'I'll just get another beer,' replied Herb, 'this is all getting too much for me but please carry on with the physics lesson.'

Oscar gritted his teeth and continued; 'Most unusually the solar wind seems to have been attracted by some force at the mine but it happened so quickly that the air pressure in the area wasn't affected and the weather carried on as normal.'

'Is this possible?' asked Emma.

'Well yes because a solar wind isn't a blowy thing as we know it. Normally it interacts with the outer atmosphere forming the ionosphere which marks our edge of space but in this instance the burst of highly changed particles punched its way through the atmospheric magnetic shield and either struck, or reacted with, a magnetic load somewhere beneath the mine.'

'Like a lightning strike?'

'Not really because lightning energy is built up from ions and whatnots that's readily available but this strike was virgin matter from way beyond and, because it's a vortex, this twister dislodged part of our normal magnetic field.'

'But there was no sign of any upheaval in the area.'

'This wasn't a physical thing as we know it. Mega trillions of iron particles around the mine were just re-magnetised ninety degrees or so off kilter.'

'And it took some time for the earth's core over-riding magnetic field to bring this renegade bit back into line again.'

'Exactly,' replied Oscar before concluding, 'and so endeth the first lesson!'

Herb had phoned his wife to say he wouldn't be home for lunch so a large take-away of fish and chips was shared amongst the four of them after which most of the questions were directed again at Oscar who ended up doing all the talking.

His enquiries regarding Jim Saidler, who was still at the psychiatric hospital in Brisbane, had not been successful as the event had happened before the army was involved. Crushing quartz has been known to send out massive jolts of electrical power so Emma and Herb were very lucky to have escaped unscathed but Jim had evidently copped quite a dose. It was likened to the Electro-Therapy treatment recently given to patients in Mental Hospitals, where most were left devoid of any soul or feeling, and Oscar didn't hold out much hope for Jim's well being.

They were all concerned about him, Emma in particular as she felt that she was the reason that they were below ground in the first place, but since none of them were close relatives they had to rely on his employers for any news which, in the present circumstances, was highly unlikely. Herb was due for another check-up at the Veterans Hospital soon so he promised to make a few enquiries of his own.

Emma asked about the reincarnate, or whatever it was that burst out of its quartz cast, and Oscar told of his frustrations with the laboratory who had done the initial testing. They had assumed that the hair sample had come from a recent head and came to their conclusions accordingly but, when a couple of boffins from Defence visited them and revealed selected facts about the sample before questioning the staff on their findings, this led to the report being amended to include an element of doubt owing to a possibility of cross contamination from the surrounding environment. This enabled Defence to then pass it through the 'Out' tray into the dead zone.

The Teleportation Theory however was different. It just wouldn't go away no matter how hard Defence tried as too many people were involved. Oscar got quite technical in his attempts to explain but eventually got most of his points over.

The Unified Field Theory, a phrase coined by Einstein, involved both Gravity and Electromagnetic Radiation but no specific formula had been found combining the two different forces so, in theory anyway, it was impossible to bend light around an object. The Philadelphia Experiment, as the incident back in 1943 was labelled, had been so mired down in controversy over the years since that it became impossible to separate the facts from the fiction. However, as with most events which fail to fit into a specific pigeonhole, this one was bandied around until the final mix bore no resemblance to the initial concoction.

Defence had no idea what they were dealing with on this specific subject so, in the absence of a rational explanation, indirect discussions between them and the mining company had agreed on a press release which, they hoped, would satisfy the growing media interest in the case of the Teleporting Japanese Mining Engineers. Once the press release was in the public domain both organisations planned to close ranks and no further statements would be issued.

There remained one aspect of water samples from the mine that Oscar was due to collect, and which he would have loved to share with the rest but couldn't. His immediate superior waxed lyrical regarding the benefits of homoeopathic medicine, being firmly convinced of the memory qualities of water, and he would personally be testing the sample to see if it could remember where it came from. Oscar hadn't enquired too deeply on how this was to be achieved but he did have great difficulty in keeping a straight face!

'So that's the stalemate at the moment and, if the feelings in my bones are anything to go by, that's where the teleporting theory will stay.' He shut his folder and slumped back into his chair. 'This will be my last visit as this particular project is winding down although I'll keep my eyes and ears open of course. They just want a final inspection so I'll do that tomorrow and then it's back to Townsville.'

Herb had other business waiting for his attention so he left and Oscar got up to follow him through the door.

'I'll try and call here on my way out of town if time permits.'

'Thanks again,' said Emma and gave him a well earned hug. 'Maybe this saga isn't ended as we do plan to drive out to the mine sometime tomorrow for a final look-see so maybe we'll meet there.'

With that Oscar picked up his briefcase and waved back to them before stepping out onto the footpath.

Chapter 31

Saffie let out a low growl as they turned off the main highway on to the unsealed road leading to the Mine. She had been down this track before, and the memories weren't good, but she had vented her feelings after which she settled down once more on the cushions.

'Thanks for this,' said Emma reaching over for Paul's hand on the steering wheel as the mirror image of the billabong eventually appeared reflected on the horizon. 'I wanted to see it one more time before the Government tries to seal it, or blow it up, or whatever they want to happen to it under the guise of *Public Safety!*'

'It's important that we try to put a closure on this so we can move on.'

'There are still so many unanswered questions though…'

'I know but don't you think we've spent enough time on it?' He paused to change down a gear then continued; 'don't get me wrong, the whole scenario has been a learning curve and I wouldn't have missed it for the world but we've come to an end. The Government, the Army, and the mining companies, we just haven't the resources, or the time, or the money, to martyr ourselves against these forces so let's call a draw. A sort of *Status Quo!*'

'I agree with what you're saying but…'

From past discussional experiences with Emma, Paul knew better than to labour a point so he left it at that and concentrated on his driving hoping that she could eventually come to terms with the whole saga.

On arrival at the site they found that the coils of barbed wire were laid out to form a tortuous path for trucks and vehicles near to the water's edge but, once they had parked by the trees, Emma and Paul could walk up between them and were soon standing on a sandbank overlooking the water.

It seemed so calm but every so often a gas bubble would break through the surface to disturb the peace and quiet.

'Just for old time's sake!' said Emma, noting the enquiring look from Paul, as she set up her audio recorder and switched it on.

'Did you absorb anything I said about putting a closure on this?'

'I know but just maybe...'

They stood quietly for a while and although they called out repeatedly for Saffie to join them, she would only condescend to sit up and peer at them out the side window. No way would she leave the security of the vehicle and soon settled down again behind the back seat.

'The water seems to cover a much larger area than just the mine;' she remarked. 'Surely the water table can't be up to this level?'

'The gas bubbles indicate that a pressure within must be supporting the level.'

'Meaning clear spaces way down below where that thing..,' she shivered involuntary at that left unsaid.

He reached out and put an arm on her shoulder. 'It was only one of Oscar's many theories that...'

A larger gas bubble burst through and the water seemed to boil momentarily.

'What temperature would the water be?'

'I'm not going to dip my toes in that's for sure,' replied Paul then continued; 'Oscar was saying about Paralina, an area somewhere north of the Flinders Ranges that's got a few really toxic hot springs. It's all very highly radio active from the nuclear fission occurring naturally below and helium gas bubbles up through the mixture. It's all very alkaline there as opposed to this water that's acidic. The temp is constant at 62 degrees and...'

The earth momentarily shook in that mid sentence and the sandbank they were standing on started to drop away rapidly towards the water's edge. Emma screamed and nearly went with it but Paul's quick thinking pulled them both over backwards and they scrambled down the slope and on towards the truck. This took some time as the barbed coils snagged their clothing at every turn and, when they touched the wire to free themselves, it delivered quite a sharp shock.

Thankfully the driver's door had been left open and Paul switched on the starting key as he scrambled in.

'God,' Emma screamed as she snatched her hand away from the passenger's door handle, 'the bloody thing's alive!'

'Climb in from this side then!'

She rushed around and in, scrambling over Paul before almost falling head first into the seat.

'I'll go to the top of the ridge,' he said slamming the door, 'and roll down towards the track if the electrics pack up again.'

'That's if the bloody thing starts,' he muttered under his breath.

'Got it,' he said when the engine fired first time.

'No! Paul!'

He was already moving off but the urgency in her voice caused him to brake hard and he turned to see the surface of the lake rising up accompanied by a heavy mist, reminiscent of a squat atomic cloud, which then blotted out the sun and plunged the area into semi darkness. After a few moments it slowly descended back to its original level and they were both momentarily transfixed by the scene that had unfolded in the rear view mirror.

'Shit!'

The engine had stopped and Paul fiddled with the key but the ignition lights remained dead; 'The bloody things conked out again.'

In the meantime Emma had managed to half open the window and was trying to open the door from the outside.

'We can't die here, not here!' she wailed in a funereal tone.

'For Christ's sake don't start any of your bloody prima donna acts,' he shouted pulling her arm over to his side, 'stay where you are and let it be for the moment.'

His plea was interrupted by a further tremor that caused them both to turn and look back. The surface of the lake had risen again, though only a metre or so this time, but soon started to settle as it took on shapes barely recognisable.

That was until it reached its original level when the shapes became very recognisable. Covered wagons and trains of oxen, initially reminiscent of the Wild West but then equally so of the mid 19th century Australian Pioneers, dominated the scene together with various horse drawn buggies and then, as the mist started to settle, a multitude of smaller shapes predominately human but including cattle, sheep and domestic animals.

The silence was deafening as the local native birds and insects all stopped their chatter. The local world seemed to be waiting for the next move from this petrified image and it came when the mist finally cleared and the sun, once again on a full beam factor, shone its warmth onto the frozen scene and the thaw began.

First there were sounds. Not from Emma and Paul, as neither could have uttered a word, but from the almost amphitheatrical performance developing before their mesmerised eyes. It was as if a sound track, from a market or crowd film shoot, had been suddenly switched on again from its pause mode. Not the sounds of a time warped package of an earlier life suddenly released from bondage but one so typical of any large group starting off on a long journey.

Buzzes of loud conversation; the cries and shouts together with the creaking and straining of mechanical joints; the animal vocals and stamping of hoofs; were all swirled into a maelstrom of sound that rose up into a crescendo of implied high expectation that identified it as a probable group from yesteryear and of an era long gone.

Moments later, as if the pause button was depressed once again, all movement froze and all sound was muted and then, just as the iron filings randomly spread on a sheet of paper align themselves towards their respective poles when a magnet is passed close by, this group aligned themselves into a proportionally neat wagon train configuration accompanied by that faint clicking sound that Emma recognised.

The tremors started again, almost like a drum roll preceding a fanfare and then, after reaching what could only be called a climatic eruption, the violence of the movement gradually receded returning the billabong water to its previous level.

What remained was a mirage of the previous image, shimmying and shadowing upon the water's surface under the harsh noonday sun, but complete in every detail except that its solidification had been replaced by an almost opaque transparency with a single exception. A tall bearded figure, attired in a dark suit and wearing a wide brimmed hat that shielded his face, appeared to be addressing the crowd from the baseboard of the leading wagon. His outfit was reminiscent of a much earlier era, as were the bonnets and hats of his audience whose upturned faces were reflected in the intense ethereal glow that surrounded the speaker and his podium. The wagon train was ready to go, that much was obvious by the horses chomping at their bits, but they held back until the figure gestured the sign of the cross before turning around and climbing into the seat beside the driver.

The intensity of the glow faded and the skies darkened as the wagons started to move off, first slowly towards the truck where Emma and Paul sat, and then speeding up before veering to the left and slowly disappearing over the horizon towards Townsville from whence they had come all those years ago.

Chapter 32

A few minutes elapsed before they became coherent again. Emma seemed to have slumped into some sort of coma while it took the same time for Paul to rationalise his thoughts and begin to wonder if the mushrooms served for breakfast might possibly have been of the hallucinogenic variety.

'Was that real or not?' each asked the other and neither seemed able to move until Emma, as if suddenly remembering her previous concerns about dying, pushed the door open intending to step out but then shut it again just as quickly.

A whirlwind, accompanied by the whoosh that rapidly increased in sound intensity, suddenly developed above the surface of the billabong and took on a plume configuration. It appeared to be sucking at the water, as if trying to drain the contents, but the water level remained constant. The clicking noise, first faint but eventually so loud that they covered their ears, seemed to reach a crescendo before dying away as the object of its efforts slowly broke free from the surface.

It was the helicopter. Not a mishmash of broken fuselage, gearbox, and rotor blades, but crisp and shining and so complete that it looked as if it had just emerged from the manufacturers. It quickly faded from view, before either Paul or Emma could take note of its colour or catch sight of any crew, but the plume surrounding the unit, coupled with the sound of an ascending propeller, swirled slowly upwards until it was out of sight and sound.

'Where's Saffie?'

'Behind the back seat,' replied Paul, 'and scared witless I shouldn't wonder.'

Emma got out and walked around the truck to open up the tailgate where she fully expected Saffie to leap into her arms but this wasn't to be.

'She's not here!'

'Christ,' he replied,' she must have jumped out but she can't have gone far.'

'I'm not leaving without Saffie…'

'For God's sake don't get too close, I don't want to lose you as well.'

He could see her from a distance, walking around the water's edge and calling the dog's name but of Saffie there was no sign.

'I can't find her,' Emma replied walking slowly back towards him.

A dusting of sand had dried on her face and the tears washed rivulets away under her eyes: 'Come and sit in the shade while we think,' he said and led her to the trees where she had first sat with Herb all those months before.

'Did we see what we saw or what?' Paul asked hoping that Emma would somehow come up with a rational explanation of the event they had just witnessed but her concerns were obviously elsewhere.

'Saffie wouldn't have gone near the water for a start,' he said hopefully.

'Why not,' answered Emma defiantly, 'she had a grand old time up at Innisfail!'

'Yes but she didn't like this area and most likely remembered the stress it caused her the last time she was here.'

'Maybe she came to see what we were up to…'

'She could have but I didn't see her.'

'Possibly the earth tremors frightened her and she's hiding somewhere?'

'Well let's concentrate on finding her then. You search central and I'll work around the outskirts.'

After an hour or so an army truck arrived to monitor the readings at the mine. Paul had made several attempts to discuss the subject of the mirages with Emma but she had the habit of being able to focus all her thoughts on one thing so, at this point in time, locating her lost dog was all that was on her mind. However they did agree not to share their earlier experience with the soldiers as it would be too difficult, and take too long, to try and explain. All available resources needed to be focused on finding the dog and the Signal Corporal, who they both knew, was in charge of the unit and soon organised his men to assist.

They searched diligently around and about and beyond for Saffie, with a halt only being called when the natural light started to fade, but there was absolutely no sign of her. The Army planned to be on site for a couple days, maybe more when it was noticed there had been further subsidence's around the water's edge, and Emma was inclined to stay but Paul persuaded her that the motel was a more comfortable and safe option. The soldiers promised to contact her if the dog turned up and they'd pass the word around to any other units in the area.

By the time they arrived back in town the animal shelters were closed. Emma insisted on contacting them anyway, although most only had answerphones on line, and Paul hadn't the heart to tell her that there was no chance that Saffie could have been handed in so soon. The police were alerted, even the local radio station which broadcast an all points bulletin and notified the Truckers FM. After this was done Emma called up her friends and relations and all Paul could do was to sit, and wait, and to keep her coffee mug topped up.

The night passed somehow, with Emma fuelled on adrenaline and Paul dropping off to sleep through sheer exhaustion. Either the phone ringing or a plea from Emma constantly disturbed him but of Saffie there were no positive leads.

The sound of movement brought him out of his deep sleep and he noted the time.

'I'd like to go back and give it another go. She must be hungry by now and to continue hiding out won't seem such a good idea.'

'Did you get any sleep at all?' he asked as he reached for his robe and walked into the bathroom.

'Are you suggesting we just leave it then?'

'I didn't say that and I can't hear you,' he called out from under the shower, 'wait until I'm finished.'

Paul took a deep breath as he towelled himself dry and then, stepping out onto the mat and putting on his wrap he answered, diplomatically: 'What I am saying is that you stay and handle things here and I'll see if either Herb or Oscar are free and if they are then we'll all go over and carry on with the search.'

At that moment there was a hammering on the door, it was Oscar; 'I heard this morning, the appeal on the radio…'

Paul pre-empted any further enquiry by asking if he could accompany him out to the mine and help in the search.

'Of course, I was going out there later on anyway but I'll have to rearrange a couple of things. We'll use my truck so hang about and I'll collect you from here.'

Emma came through and plugged in the hair dryer. She looked dreadfully tired but he knew better than to tell her so he put a couple of slices into the toaster and switched on the kettle.

'We need more milk and bread,' she said, attempting some normal conversation but her voice quickly wavered, her shoulders shook, and she started to sob. He took her in his arms but she was shaking almost violently so he led her back into the bedroom and on to the bed.

'I can't lose her,' she said between sobs, 'she's my best friend and is always there for me!'

At that moment Paul's mobile went off in the lounge and he went through. It was Herb who asked if they needed any help so, when Paul explained the situation, he offered to get his sister Meg fired up, together with her nurse friend Carol, and they'd both come over to sort Emma out.

They all arrived eventually in Oscar's truck and the two women initially tried the light-hearted approach but when they realised how deeply distressed Emma was, they both started to cry almost out of sympathy. At this point the three men, as Herb had volunteered to accompany them, decided it was time to leave so they did.

The army truck was still on site when they arrived and Saffie hadn't been seen but one of the soldiers had spotted some fresh dingo droppings early that morning.

This was not good news as wild and domestic dogs don't usually mix although blue heelers are cattle dogs and tough characters when aroused. Paul and Herb immediately started to search the outlying areas while Oscar conferred with the soldiers as he needed to take water samples from several depths together with more magnetic reading and required some assistance to do this.

They worked until lunch after which they congregated around the army truck. One of the soldiers had set up a barbeque and served quite a respectable meal of beef-burgers, onions and jacket potatoes. Paul commented, rather sadly, that if the smell of fried beef-burgers and onions didn't bring Saffie out of hiding then nothing would. When there was no retort from the rest, tears welled up in Paul's eyes and he turned away. How Emma would react, when the full effect of the dog's loss finally sunk in, he dreaded to even think about and it was with some relief that an offer by Oscar brought him back to the present.

'She may well have slipped down one of the vent holes.'

'What vent holes?' Paul asked.

'If you take this truck as one point and that anthill, the one by the broken fence, as the other point then the joining line follows, more or less, the underground water course that feeds the mine. You can hear the water gurgling in some places if you pace it out.'

Paul was just about to point out that Innisfail wasn't in that direction but, as the Corporal was also interested in what Oscar was saying, he remarked instead; 'So you think Saffie might have fallen into one?'

'Possible so I'll get the ground radar, it's an ancient model but will still track the water course, and we'll give it a go!'

It was over two hours before they finally gave up and called it a day. They had all taken it in turn to carry the ground radar, a box that weighed over eight kilos and hung most uncomfortably around the neck, but sadly they had no rescued dog to show for their labours, only a couple of old bronze ploughshears that Herb said he'd take to the local museum.

'I thought it was an old book of litmus papers, but when I got the same neutral reading with a new book I tasted the bloody stuff.'

Oscar was explaining the results as he filled in the water test sheets. 'It was sweet water with no hint of acid at all, I just don't understand it…'

'Like whatever was contaminating it just upped and left?' suggested Paul.

'Exactly that,' said Oscar, 'any ideas?'

'No,' was the reply and Paul just left it at that.

Soon afterwards the army had their gear packed and were about to leave when the Corporal walked over to offer his condolences. They thanked all the soldiers for their help and watched as they drove away in a cloud of dust.

Paul sat on the sandbank staring into the water as Oscar and Herb waited patiently in the truck. They both knew the trauma he was going through but also realised that he had to come to terms with the fact that the chances of Saffie still being alive, after all this time and in such a hostile environment, were very slim indeed. Eventually he joined them again and climbed into the back seat, clasped his hands in his lap, hung his head and remained in that position all the way back to town.

Chapter 33

The music and cheering from *The Carrington Hotel*, next door to the motel, could be heard as they turned into the main street.

'Someone must have won the lottery,' said Oscar as he pulled into the car park and continued; 'I'm going for a beer, it's been a bloody long day!'

'I'm with you on that one,' agreed Herb. 'How about you Paul?'

'I'd better break the news to Emma. I'll catch you guys later and thanks for your time.'

'I nearly forgot,' Herb said opening the boot and handing Paul a bundle wrapped in a cloth. 'A soldier found it and asked me if it belonged to Emma.'

'What is it?'

'Her audio recorder that she must have left somewhere on the site!'

They watched as he walked towards the motel then Herb stepped forward but Oscar caught his arm. 'Let him be, they'll sort it out,' and with that they both turned and walked into the Lounge Bar.

The door to number eight was ajar and Paul gingerly pushed it open. No one about and, in the bedroom, the bed had been made up and the room tidied. He walked back into the lounge, put the bundle on the table, and sat on the sofa wondering what had happened to her. The hospital scenario came to mind and then, just as a panic attack was developing, she suddenly appeared at the door.

She was swaying then smiling, then smiling broadly and singing softly;

'My dear old dog is safe and well.
Gather around and I will tell.
Of a walk she took up hill down dale.
To end right up in Innisfail!'

They drank through until the wee small hours. The local radio station, with commercial advertising paying the tab, had opened a free bar in the Carrington where the DJ actually broadcasted the programs from the beer garden. It was a party to end all parties and Saffie, in her absence, was voted on to the town council by a unanimous decision.

Nothing moved in room eight, or in the immediately vicinity, much before the late afternoon of the next day and then, for the first hour or so, it was confined mostly to the consumption of vast quantities of coffee after which Paul took a shower. As he towelled himself dry and put on his wrap, sounds drifted in from the lounge and he assumed that Emma had switched on the television but when he walked through she was leaning over, and listening intently to, the audio recorder set up on the table.

'It's been scorched on one side,' she offered by way of an explanation regarding the loudness and quality of sound, 'and the volume control is seized and the speaker damaged.'

Paul sat down beside her to listen and then commented; 'I'm certain that when the last section of the tape, when he who I assumed was the leader addressed the crowd before they finally moved off, is run through the graph recorder it will definitely indicate a speech pattern probably similar to the one we had before!'

Their return to Brisbane, via Innisfail of course, was planned to commence early the following day and they had previously decided to keep the question of the mirage to themselves as they still couldn't believe that it had actually happened. However from the evidence on the tape, confirming all the sounds of the activity that they had witnessed, no way could they just drive away and not share it with their good friends.

They were all sitting in the lounge listening to the tape on Oscar's audio recorder that he happened to have in the truck. Herb had been at home watering his vegetable patch and soon came over but Oscar was on his way back to Townsville, thankfully only twenty or so kilometres out of town and almost out of mobile phone range. He stopped and managed to pick up most of the broken message, which sounded urgent, so he turned around and drove back.

'Anyone for a beer?' asked Herb walking through to the kitchen and, when no one answered, he returned with a solitary can and opened it.

'It sounds like the track from a very old cowboy film and poses more question than it answers!'

'Well it proves that…'

'It really proves nothing my dear Emma,' interrupted Herb.

'Of course it does,' she replied leaning forward aggressively and then lying back slowly as her hangover kicked in.

'Only to us four here but who on earth else is going to believe this far-fetched fairy tale apart from maybe the alien groups and a few other weird folk.'

'But we saw what we saw and the tape is our proof!'

'I'm not doubting that, and don't forget we've got Michael McGinnis' account of the helicopter crash on disc!'

'That's a point,' remarked Oscar, 'I definitely thought that this was to be my last visit here as far as the mine is concerned but hearing that tape could well put a different slant on things.'

'What do you mean by that?' asked Herb.

'Well, if those that dwelled there before have up and left, and the water has obviously now lost whatever corrosive qualities it had, then it might be possible to retrieve the helicopter wreckage and its occupants!'

Emma sensed a slight headshake from Paul as they had previously discussed the helicopter sequence but unfortunately the tape had run out on the recorder at the time. With no audio evidence to support that particular event, and the feeling that they might well have been daydreaming, they decided not to mention it.

Until now!

'There was something else that we thought we saw but only after the tape had run out,' and Emma continued with the story but, before she could finish, Oscar interrupted her.

'The Signals are still doing radar sweeps over the area and they did pick up something on that day which they couldn't identify but it faded from their screens so fast that they didn't have time to push the panic button.'

'Do you think it could have been recorded?'

'Possibly but as no action was taken it may well have been wiped, I'll look into it anyway.'

This new information brought a lull in the conversation until Emma switched off the tape and changed the subject slightly; 'That faint clicking noise, Herbie and I heard that first time we were there, then McGinnis heard it again when the chopper fuselage was being dragged into the swamp and then on this tape when they were forming into a disciplined column ready to move on.'

'Almost as if they were using the magnetic forces to align themselves for action and taking some form of energy from it to act,' Oscar suggested.

'And don't forget that we mentioned,' Paul replied, 'that the barbed wire was delivering quite a bolt of electricity when the eruption first started. So that could have been acting like a shocking coil by picking up the stray magnetic currents!'

'Oh my God,' exclaimed Emma putting her hands up to her cheeks, again rather theatrically, before slumping forward.

The others exchanged glances but said nothing.

'I've gone all goosebumply!'

'Don't you mean goosepimply?' asked Herb unable to resist a repartee.

'These are definitely bumps, believe me, as I've just thought. What if that clicking noise we heard that first time was them aligning themselves ready for action and we were the target.'

Even Herb went a shade puce at that revelation and they sat in silence until Paul asked: 'So where does that leave us then?'

'Not much further along the track I'm afraid but that's about all we can do with it for the moment,' replied Oscar supporting Herb's initial argument.

'So that's it then as far as you two are concerned?'

'Leave it Emma,' warned Paul and with that she jumped up and ran into the garden where she slumped down under one of the shade trees.

Oscar looked at his watch and stood up. He could see a heated discussion brewing, and he wanted to be on his way before it erupted, but he had one last question before he left.

'I've got to go but what happened to Saffie?'

The finale!

Paul had managed to hear a garbled explanation of the dog's reappearance into the material world and so, after a shower, he had sat Emma down to explain the sequence of events.

Rachel had been cycling from work, on the afternoon Saffie had gone missing, when she saw the dog playing with her Alsatian friend. She assumed that Emma was somewhere nearby and assumed the same when Saffie was waiting outside the cafe the next morning. It wasn't until that lunchtime, with the dog happily sleeping in the sun and no sign of Emma, that alarm bells rang and she decided to phone. Rachel rang the mobile number and was most surprised that Emma answered from Charters Towers. She sounded so relieved that Saffie had been found, and even more relieved when Rachel assured her that the dog would be no trouble to look after until she could collect her. After Rachel hung up she began to wonder how Saffie had travelled so far, and reached the conclusion that she must have hitched a ride going north and got off, remembering the delicious scraps she had had in the *Tregrosse Café*, at the beach above Innisfail!

Sheer luck, Emma agreed later with Rachel, and left it at that.